Come Dance With Me

Come Dance With Me

RUSSELL HOBAN

BLOOMSBURY

First published in Great Britain 2005

Copyright © 2005 by Russell Hoban

The moral right of the author has been asserted

Bloomsbury Publishing Plc, 38 Soho Square, London WID 3HB

A CIP catalogue record for this book is available from the British Library

ISBN 0 7475 7452 9

10 9 8 7 6 5 4 3 2 1

Typeset by Palimpsest Book Production Limited, Polmont, Stirlingshire

Printed in Great Britain by Clays Ltd, St Ives plc

'Hawaii '78' by Israel Kamakawiwo'ole © Bigboy Record Company.
Reprinted by permission of Mountain Apple and the estate of
Israel Kamakawiwo'ole.

'Freight Train' by Sonny Terry and Brownie McGhee ℗ 1959 Fantasy Inc.
Reprinted by permission of Pru Music Publishing.

'The Worms at Heaven's Gate' by Wallace Stevens is from
The Collected Poems of Wallace Stevens © 1954 by Wallace Stevens and
renewed 1982 by Holly Stevens. Used by permission of Alfred A. Knopf,
a division of Random House, Inc. and by Faber & Faber Ltd.

'Linger Awhile' ℗ 1962 Capitol Records Inc. © 1923 Leo Feist Inc.,
USA (50%) EMI United Partnership Ltd. (Print rights controlled by
Warner Bros. Publications Inc./IMP Ltd.) Reproduced by permission of
International Music Publications Ltd. All right reserved.
Words by Larry Owens, music by Vincent Rose.

Lines lettered on Django's coffin are from *Myths and Legends of Hawaii*,
re-told by W.D. Westervelt, published by Mutual Publishing Co of
Honolulu, Hawaii © 1987

'Now's the Time to Fall in Love (Potatoes Are Cheaper, Tomatoes
Are Cheaper)', De Sylva, Brown and Henderson, 1931.
Words and music by Al Sherman and Al Lewis.

ACKNOWLEDGEMENTS

If the goodwill and hours and miles of help I had on this novel were laid end to end they would reach from here to Kahakuloa Head.

Andrew Bown of Status Quo was my consultant and guide in all musical matters and gave me encyclopaedic data.

Nunu Whiting and Dave Salt let me visit Waterloo Sunset rehearsal studios and Claire Ferris gave me a complete tour.

Ben Schlapak, Manager of Honolulu International Airport, graciously authorised my enquiries and sent me useful descriptions. Jenny Hausler of the Visitors' Information Office reported on the gardens and the now-closed Mini Hotel.

Emmae Gibson, like me, went through Honolulu International Airport in 1993 and generously shared her impressions.

Dennis Camblin of Hawaii spent days travelling in Maui on my behalf. He sent me voluminous notes and hundreds of photographs as well as books, maps and pressed flowers.

Graeme Wend-Walker provided detailed notes, photographs, and diagrams of Los Angeles International Airport.

Susan Ruskin gave me her current observations of LAX.

Rob Warren of the Greenwich Observatory supplied astronomical data.

Dr Michael Feher of Chelsea & Westminster Hospital was my consultant in diabetic matters.

Dr Ben Hoban answered general medical questions.

Liz Calder, Katherine Greenwood, Phoebe Hoban and Dominic Power gave useful comments.

Gundula, my wife, translated 'Der Tod und das Mädchen' on pp. 28–29 and 'Herr Oluf' on p. 32. She also kept me up to date with London in general and fashions in particular.

Two *National Geographic* articles were valuable sources: 'Hawai'i: Preserving the Breath' by Paul Theroux, December 2002 and 'Maui: Where Old Hawaii still Lives' by Kenneth F. Weaver, April 1971.

The ANAPAESTS FOR PEACE T-shirt was derived from Neil Bennett's cartoon in the 1 May 2001 edition of *The Times*.

The Daniel Mendoza and Coffee As You Like It are fictional.

The European free-tailed bat who crash-landed on p. 100 was rescued by Ginni Little of the Cornwall Bat Hospital. Now rejoicing in the name of Hobbit Higgins (because of his hairy feet), he is thriving under Mrs Little's care. The Cornwall Bat Hospital has no income other then private donations and the money it receives from its adoption scheme. Ginni Little's work with these fascinating creatures deserves all possible support.

R.H.
London, 23 July 2004

To the memory of Lillian Hoban

'Life has surprises. Life is absurd.
Because it is absurd, there is always hope.'

Graham Greene, *The Honorary Consul*

'It's free but it ain't cheap.'

Robert Duvall, *The Apostle*

CONTENTS

CHRISTABEL ALDERTON

21 January 2003. I read somewhere that a butterfly flapping its wings in Hong Kong could affect the course of a tornado in Texas. Sure, why not? Probably the first time I put on mascara I made it rain in Norwich three years later and Dick Turpin fall off a roof a year and a half after that. I don't need a scientist to tell me that everything's connected and a teentsy cause in one place can result in a big effect some other place. Chaos Theory is what they call it, which is the right name for any theory that concerns me. Life is full of problems, you have to expect that, but I have this extra thing that gives me trouble.

I was thirteen the first time it happened. We lived in High Hill Ferry by the River Lea, that's in Upper Clapton. Across the river the view is very wide. Over the Walthamstow Marshes the sky is big, everything else is small. Beyond the railway the sheds, pylons, gantries and distant buildings are all very small under the sky.

It was in August: 7 August 1962, I wrote the date in my diary. I was walking by the river. The banks were all purple with Michaelmas daisies and there were moorhens nesting in the reeds. The sky was blue, the sun was warm, the shadows were cool in the tunnel under the railway bridge. Beyond the bridge the river stretched away all calm and peaceful into the distance. A boat came along, a big cabin cruiser, the *Badroulbadour*. The name reminded me of a princess in *The Arabian Nights*, Badoura, but this name had a different feel to it. There were a lot of people on the boat and some of them waved to me. As I looked the action seemed to freeze for a moment and it was like a photograph of people waving. 'Better not,' I said. Not loud enough for them to hear me. Why did I say that? The picture unfroze and the boat and the people passed out of my view while I stood there shaking my head and feeling strange.

After tea my stepfather went to The Anchor & Hope for his usual four pints and later on I went out too. I liked that time of evening when the lamps were lit and the sky was still light, it sometimes gave me good ideas for the poems I wrote in my diary. I saw a bat flittering about and tossed up a pebble. The bat followed it down for a moment but its sonar must have told it pebbles are no good to eat so it flew off into the dusk.

I didn't ordinarily go near the pub in the evening when Ron, my stepdad, was there. But there were men on the benches outside The Anchor & Hope and

I wanted to hear what they were talking about. They were all local and I knew some of them. When I got close enough to hear them Ted Wilmot was saying, 'I was at the marina when I heard it blow up. You could see the smoke and flames from half a mile away. Killed all nine people.'

Without thinking I said, 'The *Badroulbadour?*' Everybody turned to look at me.

'That's the one, Chrissy,' said Mr Wilmot. 'Did you know anybody on board?'

'No,' I said. I started to cry and I ran home. I knew that I was somehow connected to the deaths of those people, but how? When I said, 'Better not,' I wasn't foreseeing anything, the words just came out of my mouth. I went up to my room and wrote what happened in my diary but I had no poems in me that evening. When Ron got back from the pub he came stomping up the stairs so the whole house shook and it was about a six-pint smell that came ahead of him. He flung the door open without knocking as he always did but I was used to this and I was fully dressed. 'Piss off, Ron,' I said.

'I know for a fact you were in all afternoon,' he said. 'How'd you know about the *Badroulbadour?*'

'I've got second sight,' I said. 'Want me to tell you what's going to happen to you?'

His eyes got very big and he went pale and hurried out of the room. He died of a stroke a year later. I couldn't see his future, I was only trying to scare him because he was a creep and I hated him.

When school started again I asked the English teacher, Mr Burton, about the name Badroulbadour. He was a short man who wasn't fat but his shirts always seemed about to pop their buttons. He smelled of sweat and aftershave and when he talked to you his hands always seemed about to touch you in various places but he pulled them back before they did. I guess he was about forty.

'You're thinking about the boat that blew up?' he said.

'Yes.' I backed away a little because of his breath.

'It's a variant of the name of the *Arabian Nights* princess Budur or Badr-al-Budur,' he said, 'and it's from a poem by Wallace Stevens, "The Worms at Heaven's Gate".' He took a book out of his desk and read:

> Out of the tomb, we bring Badroulbadour,
> Within our bellies, we her chariot.
> Here is an eye. And here are, one by one,
> The lashes of that eye and its white lid.
> Here is the cheek on which that lid declined,
> And, finger by finger, here, the hand,
> The genius of that cheek. Here are the lips,
> The bundle of the body and the feet.
>
> Out of the tomb we bring Badroulbadour.

I almost said, 'That's gross,' but I didn't because it gave me goose pimples. There was nobody else in the room but the two of us. I remember the smell of the chalk dust and the distant voices and footsteps in the halls. 'Worms,' I said, 'carrying her off in their bellies.'

'That's it,' he said. 'This beauty who was the Moon of Moons, to this favour did she come at last. This book is his collected poems. There's a copy of it in the library.'

'Have you got a boat?' I said.

'No.'

'If you had one, would you call it *Badroulbadour*?'

'No. Are you thinking of naming a boat?'

'No,' I said. 'Thank you, I'll look for the book.' I got it out of the library and read the poem. It put horrible pictures in my mind, the worms bringing out an eye and the eyelashes one by one and the eyelid. I wished I hadn't read it but it gave me a kind of thrill that made me ashamed. I leafed through the book and page after page grabbed me with ideas and images I never would have thought of, like, 'The bird kept saying that birds had once been men, / Or were to be . . .' With my birthday money I bought a copy for myself and although a lot of it was way over my head and still is, the crazy reality of his poems seems to me a realer way of seeing the world than what you get on the 'Six O'Clock News'.

The main thing on my mind back then was the blowing up of the *Badroulbadour*. Is there such a thing as luck? Most people think so, you even hear it said that some are born lucky, and being lucky is better than being rich. Was *Badroulbadour* an unlucky name to give a boat? I thought it was. When I said, 'Better not,' what exactly did I mean? Better not stay on that boat? I guess so. So maybe I really *did* have second sight, and from then on every time I had a weird feeling of any kind I expected something awful to happen but it didn't work that way. Sometimes a bad thing happened and sometimes it didn't, so I was never sure and I was always uneasy. Still am. I came to think that maybe I was just bad luck. I kept it all to myself and hoped that it would go away. I made friends and tried to lead a normal life and nothing happened for a long time.

I didn't mean to get into all that right now. I should be getting my head around doing my thing yet again at the Hammersmith Apollo this Friday. I've never been very dignified but I'm getting too old to climb out of a body drawer while the crew do Hammer Horror effects with dry ice. Mobile Mortuary is the name of the band and I've climbed out of that drawer in a lot of places I wouldn't mind never seeing again. In some of them the dressing rooms smell about the same as the toilets and the sink is the safest place to pee. I have to knock back a little vodka to get my voice straight and the guys in the band use up the same amount of liniment, painkillers, and knee and elbow bandages as a football team but we still make money and they love us in Tirana. So it's hard to stop but it really isn't me any more, I'm not who I was when I started rocking around various clocks. What else is new.

When I'm not working my life is quieter than it

used to be. Last year I became a patron of the Royal Academy of Arts and I've been buying art books. When I discovered Goya's etchings I felt like starting a new band and calling it *Los Caprichos*. I didn't though. Sometimes I find pictures that were already in my head or they seem to have been: various lithographs by Odilon Redon especially. There are all kinds of things it would be better not to see and he's drawn as many of them as he could. Sometimes when I look at those lithographs I feel a bit queasy. It's as if he knows something about me that he oughtn't to know. Crazy thought. He's been dead since 1918. So far I haven't read anything about his life but I think there must have been a lot of blackness in it. His lithographs are called The Blacks, *Les Noirs*. Up to the evening I'm about to describe I had only that one book of Redon's work.

Today I was at a private view of 'The Symbolists' at the Royal Academy and all of a sudden there was a painting by Redon, *The Cyclops*. I'd never seen any of his paintings, not even reproductions. Looking at this one I felt that I'd seen that cyclops before. Had I been to that place in dreams where I smell the salt wind and the sea? The naked woman lying there, maybe she's been left as a sacrifice – is it me? She has her arms raised as if to ward off the stare of this huge creature that's peeping over the edge of where she is, a monstrous misshapen head with one giant eye in the centre of it and a disgusting little mouth that you don't want to think about. Or maybe she's accepting it, opening her arms to it, I didn't know, I couldn't be sure about the woman and the cyclops.

There were a lot of people between me and the painting and I hadn't yet finished looking at it when I noticed a man watching me from about ten feet away. Not a Mobile Mortuary fan, I thought. He was tall, nice-looking, definitely interested, and about fifteen to twenty years older than I used to pull. Well, the years are going by faster all the time, aren't they. I had to smile, not at him, but because I was thinking that his taste in women was as unreliable as mine in men.

The people between me and *The Cyclops* were gone and I had a clear view of it again and stepped closer. It's only about two feet high but it suddenly opened up and became huge in front of me. I was in a big silence and then I thought I could hear the sea far below me. 'Oh,' I said, as if I suddenly knew something that I hadn't known before. Then the room started to spin and I just made it down to the ladies' in time to throw up.

I was still shaky when I went back to the exhibition. I didn't see Mr Interested but I wasn't really in the mood for making new friends anyhow so that was OK. I didn't look at *The Cyclops* again and I avoided Redon altogether. There were some good Bresdins that didn't make me vomit and of course Moreau and Böcklin and others that I now know as the usual suspects in Symbolist art.

There were drinks after the show and a lot of champagne was being put away by people with money to spend on the arts. The catering staff, all young and all in black, kept topping me up and I kept emptying my glass, so I was feeling pretty free and easy by the time I bumped into Mr Interested or he bumped into me. He'd had enough bubbly to put a little heart into him and this time he smiled at me.

I said to him, '*Komm tanze mit mir!*' What in the world made me say that? I remember that I had to grab his arm because I almost fell over. Champagne doesn't do that to me, it must have been the vodka I'd had before coming to the Royal Academy, although I'd have thought my session in the ladies' would have given me a clean slate. '*Komm tanze mit mir!*' Did I say it twice?

He seemed surprised. 'Are you German?' he said.

'No,' I said. 'Are you?'

'Half – my mother is. That's a line from 'Herr Oluf'. Why did you say it to me?'

'I don't know, I'm not responsible for everything I say.'

'Are you the Erlking's daughter?'

'Maybe, but I don't feel like dancing now. Anyhow, this is not a dancing situation, it's a Symbolists do and symbols refer to something else. Like me.'

'What do you refer to?'

'Different things at different times. I have to pee.' Off I went. I hung around the loo for a long time thinking about the line I'd quoted from 'Herr Oluf'. It's a Loewe ballad and 'Come dance with me' is what the Erlking's daughter says to Herr Oluf as he's riding late and far to summon guests to his wedding the next day. '*Komm tanze mit mir,*' she sings. He turns her down and on his wedding day he's dead. I heard that ballad for the first time in Vienna at Adam Freund's flat when he sang it to me stark naked. A weird guy, that Adam. What made me say those words to this stranger? It was as if there was a connection between us before we'd ever met. I was sort of spooked by that and I didn't know how I felt about talking to him again.

I thought I heard a man's footsteps approaching so I ducked into a cubicle. Mine was the only one that was occupied. There was a knocking at the door of the loo, and when he got no answer he came to my cubicle and said, 'Are you all right?'

I said, 'Yes, but I can't talk any more tonight.'

'When can I see you again?' he said.

You'll be sorry, I thought. 'Write down your name and slip it under the door,' I said. 'I'll call you.'

'I don't know *your* name,' he said.

'Not now,' I said. 'I'll call you.' Why was I doing this? I don't know, I do a lot of stupid things. A scrap of paper came under the door: 'Elias Newman' and his phone number.

'I'll leave you to it,' he said, and his footsteps walked away.

When I came out the lobby was pretty empty. I got my things and went outside. The air was cold and seemed heavy with snow that was almost ready to fall. I walked across the forecourt, under the arch, over the road and hailed a taxi. Piccadilly was full of lights and traffic, with a lot of blackness around the lights. When we turned into Park Lane the cars rushing through it looked as if they were emptying London; soon there'd be no more people, only driverless cars hurrying into the night. The trees in Hyde Park were pale under the lamps, with cold black shadows. Bayswater Road stared at me as if I were a foreigner. When we got to my place in Notting Hill the street was deserted, the lamps were dim. I'd left lights on in my house but they looked like lights in an empty house. I could hear a helicopter quite close, then farther away, then close again. My cat Stevo came out to meet me and we went inside together. Before I closed the door I looked back at the street and it was like a photograph of something that was gone. I shook my head and locked the door. I didn't think I'd be phoning Elias Newman.

2

ELIAS NEWMAN

21 January 2003. '*Komm tanze mit mir!*' In those words I heard my mother's voice and saw the alders and birches of the Teufelsmoor near the Worpswede of her childhood. 'On little islands in the swamps grew these trees,' she told me. 'Very slender and modest, those alders and birches. Shy they were, didn't like to be looked at. They had their own way of listening to the voices of the wind; thinly they took the light, they made small shadows on the water and the reeds and the boggy ground. Always was I very careful, very respectful there.

'One very cold Christmas Day I found a man lying dead in the shallow water where he had fallen through the ice. Hung around his neck was his camera. He was a house guest of one of the artists who lived nearby. He had no wounds, the police didn't know how he had died. I think he was foolish to photograph those very shy trees with their little shadows.'

'Did someone have the film developed? Maybe his photographs showed how he died.'

'I don't know what happened to the film.'

'How do you think he died?'

'Perhaps the Erlking's daughter reached out her hand and invited him to dance, not? Listen to this!' She sang me 'Herr Oluf', accompanying herself on the accordion and giving me shivers of dread and delight. She was beautiful, my mother, tall and elegant. She wore her fair hair in a Louise Brooks 'Lulu' bob, not a style you saw very often in our town. Her voice was thrilling, and altogether there was something mythological about her. Her name is Anneliese, and I don't know where she is now. When I was eleven she ran off with a tenor from a Pittsburgh opera company and became the myth of Anneliese. But that was still ahead, of us when she first sang 'Herr Oluf' to me. I was eight then and more of a rationalist than I am now. 'Is that song like a fairy tale?' I said.

'I don't know what to call it,' she said.

'But do you believe in the Erlking?'

'The birches and the alders on the Teufelsmoor, in them lives something. You give it a name or you don't. Now I must make supper.'

My mother when she sang to me was younger than this woman saying '*Komm tanze mit mir!*' and seeming for a moment to be speaking in my mother's voice. Green eyes this one had, red lips, pale, pale skin, pale hair. Cold and beautiful, like sparkling snow, frozen rivers, alders and birches sheathed in ice. Very slender, wearing a silvery top that was all tiny pleats, floaty and clingy at the same time. Wide silvery trousers the same. Silver boots with high heels. In her middle fifties, I thought, lit from within by that craziness that keeps some people young. Famous? Certainly she was used to being looked at. Had I seen her before tonight? I was drawn to her from the moment I saw her in front of *The Cyclops*. She didn't stand absolutely still, there were always people getting between her and it – she'd step back and then move forward again to restore the connection. I could see that the painting had a powerful effect on her. I began to think that perhaps she felt herself to be that woman lying there naked, entering the dream of the cyclops and submitting to it. I felt, with a thrill of empathy, how it was with her and it excited me; I wanted to take her in my arms and feel her trembling against me. Then she suddenly seemed to be overwhelmed, she turned away abruptly and fled.

When I saw her again it was at drinks time after the exhibition. The room was crowded with men of means and women of the serious-acquisition class, either as found or expertly restored. Among us, elegant in black, passed the catering staff symbolising the transience of youth and beauty as they dispensed champagne, sushi, wonton dip, vegetable rolls, and smiles. The silvery green-eyed woman, as found, was standing in front of me, leaning towards me. '*Komm tanze mit mir!*' she said. She leaned closer, held my arm to keep from falling and said again, '*Komm tanze mit mir!*'

I was surprised that she knew 'Herr Oluf' and even more surprised that she'd singled me out to say those words to. I asked her if she was German – she wasn't – she asked me if I was, and we got into a rather odd little conversation which she broke off to go to the loo. She was gone a long time, and in her absence I mentally replayed the action from my first sight of her in front of *The Cyclops*. Certainly it's a powerful painting and I had responded strongly to her response to it. But had she found it nauseating? She'd rushed off with her hand to her mouth the way people do when they're about to vomit. This time she'd said she had to pee but I was beginning to wonder about her bladder.

After a while the drinks table was cleared and people were queueing up to collect their things at the cloakroom, so I went to the ladies' to look for her and we had another odd little conversation through a cubicle door. Not the sort of thing I ordinarily do but I couldn't let go of the specialness of our meeting. She allowed me to slip my name and phone number under the door, wouldn't tell me her name, and said she'd phone me.

Near the cloakroom I found Peter Diggs and Amaryllis whom I'd first met at one of Peter's shows at the Nikolai Chevorski gallery. Amaryllis has been called 'the Waterhouse nymph' by Peter because she could have posed for any one of that Victorian master's many enchantresses. She teaches piano and is said to be very good at it; in her unpianistic hours she has long since come out as a weirdo. 'What did you think of the show?' she said.

'Terrific,' I said. 'I've never seen that many Redons and there were Bresdins that I never knew about.'

'I saw you talking to Christabel Alderton,' said Peter. 'Do you know her?'

'Christabel Alderton!' I said. '*That's* why I thought I might have seen her before. I don't know her at all, never met her until just a little while ago. She used to sing with . . .' I was trying to remember the band. 'Death on Speed?'

'Mobile Mortuary,' said Amaryllis. 'They don't do as many gigs in this country as they used to but they're at the Hammersmith Apollo this Friday.'

We chatted for a bit about Peter's new show. The theme was 'Death and the Maiden' and most of the paintings had red dots stuck on the frames when I turned up to have a look. Death was a beautiful pale young man, naked and mostly in shadow so that you could never quite make out how well endowed he was although he left them for dead; all the maidens were variations of Amaryllis and they were naked too. Maidens to die for, one might almost say. DEATH NEVER HAD IT SO GOOD was the headline of Noah Thawle's review in the *Guardian*.

I'd heard from our mutual friend Seamus Flannery that Peter had gone through a dry spell after Amaryllis moved in with him. 'Too much happiness,' said Seamus. 'He lost his empty spaces for a while. But with Amaryllis he's always in a state of uncertainty so he got his empties back. The consensus is that Amaryllis will stay beautifully weird for a very long time, so Peter can look forward (with or without her) to a good stretch of productivity.'

We went our separate ways then and I was alone in the cold with my thoughts and questions about Christabel Alderton. The lights of Piccadilly shining through the entrance arch made moony glimmers on the little fountain puddles in the Royal Academy forecourt. I started walking to Green Park tube station and a 19 bus loomed hugely as it dopplered towards me symbolising the mystery of redness. The Burlington Arcade, bereft of Christmas lights, sat like Patience on a monument, waiting for the next wave of tourists with strong currency. Across the road, spotlit Grecian columns of a used-to-be bank rose augustly from China House restaurant. The Ritz Hotel, also spotlit, stood with the ghosts of Januarys past, holding its place in the winter night above the swarming headlights, the roar of traffic and the rush of time. Everything seemed to refer to something else, and in my head Christabel Alderton the Erlking's daughter sang me past green banks and dancing elves, down Piccadilly to the tube station, not with 'Herr Oluf' but with two violins, a viola and a cello and the music of the Schubert Quartet No. 14, 'Death and the Maiden'. SHARES PLUNGE AGAIN, said the headline on the *Evening Standard* kiosk.

I took the Piccadilly line to Earl's Court, where

people on the platform seemed more watchful than they used to be, or maybe I was. When the train came there were plenty of seats. I sat next to a sleek young man who was reading a piece on *The Times* COMMENT page headed THE UNITED STATES OF AMERICA HAS GONE MAD, by John le Carré. His mobile rang. 'Hi, Jeremy,' he said. 'Sorry I didn't ring you back, it was just one thing after another all day.' Pause. He lowered his voice. 'Well, are you surprised? Don't you watch the Footsie and the Dow Jones?' Pause. 'Yes, I know. But that was then, this is now. "You gotta know when to hold, know when to fold, etc."' Pause. 'Well, yes, I'm sorry too. Ciao.' He shook his head and went back to John le Carré.

By then I was feeling very American and very defensive. I am, after all, a US citizen. I didn't want a war with Iraq but I wouldn't have minded if John le Carré were to be given a one-way ticket to Baghdad.

When I came out of the Underground at Fulham Broadway I heard a helicopter very close, then farther away, then close again. I looked up but couldn't see it. I walked to my house, and when I got inside I saw *The Sunday Times* on the kitchen table where I'd left it folded back to the page on which was a famous photograph that had first appeared in *Picture Post* in 1938: two girls on a rollercoaster. The skirt of the pretty blonde on the right had flown up to flash her stockinged legs, suspenders, knickers and a bit more. When I looked more closely I saw that her right hand was inside the skirt, lifting it. In one of my books there's an old engraving of a young woman putting the Devil to flight by doing that very thing. The girl in the photograph was clearly glad to be alive and confident of giving pleasure to everybody while embarrassing the Devil. Under that section of the paper was the front page of last Saturday's *Times* with a photograph of another young woman, a Navy guard with a rifle and radio and the Union Jack fluttering behind her, patrolling HMS *Ark Royal* as it took on supplies at Portsmouth before heading for the Gulf. She looked utterly reliable but I doubted that her rifle and HMS *Ark Royal* would rout the Devil more effectively than the girl on the rollercoaster. That girl would be in her eighties now.

On the coffee table in the living room was a hospital directive that I still hadn't read through: IN THE EVENT OF CHEMICAL OR BIOLOGICAL ATTACK. My mind was singing, 'Tomatoes are cheaper, potatoes are cheaper, / Now's the time to fall in love . . .' Back in the forties my father used to sing that song from the thirties. Tomatoes and potatoes must cost thirty or forty times what they did back then. He also sometimes sang, 'I Love To Spend This Hour with You', the theme song of the Eddie Cantor radio show. All his hours are long gone now.

I poured myself some Courvoisier, sat down on the sofa, took my shoes off and put my feet up on the coffee table. As I drank, the cognac gave me a warm centre, only a very small part of the world but better than nothing. I knew that Christabel Alderton was going to stay in my mind but I didn't think she was likely to phone me.

3

CHRISTABEL ALDERTON

22 January 2003. Why had I brought the Erlking into the Royal Academy? Or did he find his own way there? I thought of *The Cyclops* and I almost threw up again. Why? I don't know. Sometimes I get tired of being me. When I said that line from 'Herr Oluf' to Elias Newman I was attracted to him but at the same time I think I wanted to warn him off. Of course he wouldn't have taken it as a warning if he hadn't known the song. And somehow I knew he *would* know it. How's that for weird? Being me is confusing, and as I've said, I do a lot of stupid things.

And that dialogue in the loo! I don't know how to be with civilians any more. I'm OK with the guys in the band and my cat Stevo. He doesn't travel with the band but he's a rocker too. He's a good-looking orange-and-white tom, tiger-striped. He stinks up the place a little with his spray and he's gone for days on end and comes back looking the worse for wear but I'd never have him neutered. We understand each other. My neighbours Victor and Hal look after him when I'm away and when I get back he comes out to meet me, tail sticking up with a crook in it like an umbrella handle, and he runs up the steps ahead of me and waits at the door with his engine idling like an E-type.

The day after the Royal Academy do I was still thinking about last night's conversation and I wanted to listen to 'Herr Oluf' but I couldn't find my Hermann Prey recording of Loewe ballads. I spent a lot of time looking for it and the day was beginning to slide out from under me so I rang up HMV at Oxford Circus and they had one copy. 'Please hold it for me,' I said. 'I'll be right over.' But when I got there I was told that although the CD had appeared on the screen it was gone before it could be put aside for me. Thinking I might go for something else I went to the Hermann Prey section and there was, you guessed it, Elias Newman.

'Hello,' he said, 'this is a lot better than a phone call.' He showed me *Loewe Balladen* sung by Hermann Prey. 'Don't tell me you were looking for this too?'

'I was, actually.'

'Have this one. My treat. I'll find another some-where.'

'What is this, anyhow? Am I following you or are you sending mental messages to me?'

'Relax. I guess our conversation last evening made us both think of this recording. That's not surprising, is it?' He had blue eyes and an air of always telling the truth. A quality that I tend to back away from because it usually causes trouble.

'You might be a little too strange for me,' I said. 'You said your mother's German. Did she sing "Herr Oluf" to you?'

'I'll tell you about it,' he said. 'Come have a coffee with me.'

'OK,' I said. 'If you're hell-bent on dancing I won't stop you.' He paid for the Loewe and I took his arm as we left HMV. What is this? I thought as my breast made contact with his arm and I felt him being aware of it. Are we suddenly a couple? It felt good and it felt strange. Don't be ridiculous, I told myself as we crossed the road to Coffee As You Like It. The waitresses all wear doublet and hose and the cups have Shakespeare quotations. There's a forest of potted trees and the January daylight came through the leaves as if it didn't know that Oxford Street was on the other side of the glass. The coffee smelled good, the crockery made a cheerful rattle, and the background voices came forward and drew back like distant surf. Very atmospheric and no dry ice although I was in black leather and looking as if I'd just crawled out of a box of Transylvanian earth and jumped on my Kawasaki. He was wearing jeans and a black polo neck and some kind of army surplus jacket but he didn't look as if he dressed that way very often. Too respectable maybe. I had espresso, he had caffe latte. His cup said, 'O, how full of briers is this working-day world!'

'Maybe they're trying to warn you about me,' I said.

I asked our waitress (the name on her badge was Rosalind), 'Did you choose these cups?'

She shook her head. She had long fair hair and it swung across her face in a way that wasn't wasted on Elias. 'They take them from under the counter as they come,' she said. 'I don't see them until they fill them and put them on my tray.'

I watched her walk away and so did Elias. But he was also watching me. 'What?' he said.

'They must hire these girls for their legs. She's got no right to be so young and beautiful.'

'Shit happens. You're not young but you're beautiful.'

'Do me a favour, don't insult me with crap compliments,

OK?'

'It wasn't crap – you don't know how you look to me but OK, no more compliments. What does *your* saucer say?'

' "'Sweet are the uses of adversity, / " ' I read ' "'Which, like the toad, ugly and venomous, / Wears yet a precious jewel in its head.'"

'Tell me about your adversity,' he said.

'Not on the first date. How old are you, Elias?'

'Wait a minute, I don't know what to do on dates.'

'Sorry, I didn't mean to frighten you. It's not a date but how old are you?'

'Sixty-two. What about you?'

'Fifty-four. You haven't asked my name.'

'You're Christabel Alderton. I knew the name but

24

I'd never seen you. Some friends told me who you were. You're famous.'

'More than some, less than others. What do you do?'

'I'm a doctor.'

'What kind?'

'Diabetes consultant at St Eustace.'

'You don't act like a doctor.'

'That's because I haven't got your folder in front of me.'

'Good – you'd find it a dead boring read.'

'I doubt that. When I first saw you at the Royal Academy I was curious about you but I wouldn't have taken you for a rocker.'

'Why not? Mick Jagger's older than I am.'

'I wasn't thinking of your age – it's just that you look more like the Erlking's daughter. Which you said you were, if you recall. Are you married?'

'Was. You?'

'No.'

'Gay?'

'Melancholy, actually. Have you got any children?'

'No. You were going to tell me about your mother and "Herr Oluf".'

'My mother used to sing some of the Loewe ballads and accompany herself on the accordion. She was, is, from Worpswede which is on the Weser. There's a place called the Teufelsmoor near the town, the Devil's Moor. That's where she imagined Herr Oluf riding late at night through the birches and alders and boggy places. She acted the song out and she made me see it all, the trees and the elves and the Erlking's daughter. When she sang it she used different voices for the Erlking's daughter and Herr Oluf. One Christmas Day she found a dead man in the Teufelsmoor.'

'Was it Herr Oluf?'

'No, just somebody's house guest.'

'Did you like hearing your mother tell you about that dead man?'

'Yes. No one knew how he died, and mysterious deaths are always interesting.'

'You said your mother was, then you said she is. Is she was or is she is?'

'I don't know. She left us when I was eleven and I haven't heard from her since.'

'Left you for . . . ?'

'A tenor in a Pittsburgh opera company. I saw him once when he came to the house. He was a little puffed-up man who looked as if he could be depended on to be undependable. I couldn't imagine what my mother saw in him but she packed a bag, left a note and that was it.'

'What did the note say?'

'It said, "This is a wrong move but I must make it. Do not forgive me. That would be too much."'

'Singers.'

'Singers what?'

'I don't know.' I was thinking about Adam Freund who'd sung me 'Herr Oluf' in Vienna, a guy whose lean and slightly crazy looks of course attracted me.

Freund means friend and he was very friendly. He was singer and guitarist with Sayings of Confucius, our support band. We chatted a little and our pheromones got entangled and I said OK when he offered to show me the Belvedere and its paintings. I was sleeping with our lead guitarist at the time, Sid Horstmann, and he was more than a little pissed off but I wasn't too bothered about it. After rehearsal at the Metropol Adam walked me through various streets commenting on the architecture and all the caryatids holding up shops, banks, office buildings and blocks of flats. 'These stone women, they never quit,' he said. 'They're all big and strong and they're more reliable for holding up buildings than men are.'

My feet were beginning to hurt by the time we got to Prinz-Eugen-Strasse and started up the long hill to the palaces and gardens. In front of the Upper Belvedere there are two stone sphinxes overlooking the gardens and the Lower Belvedere. They're larger than people-size, they have wings, very serious dignified faces and very raunchy haunches. It was a cold March day but there were a lot of people about and some of them stared at Adam when he climbed up behind one of the sphinxes and pretended to be humping her. I tried to look as if I wasn't with him. 'These sphinxes turn me on,' he said as he tried to move her tail out of the way, 'but they don't know how to let themselves go.'

'Maybe she's more receptive after midnight,' I said. We went into the galleries and saw paintings by Klimt and Knopfler and Schiele. The one that really got to me was Schiele's *Death and the Maiden*. I can still see it when I close my eyes. The maiden is a big sturdy girl who looks well past her maidenhood, she might even be pregnant. She's sprawling into Death's arms, her eyes are open and she seems to be thinking, 'What the hell, why not?' Death's right hand is clutching her left shoulder and his left hand is pressing her head against his chest. Maybe he's kissing her hair. I think he is.

'Come away from there,' said Adam. 'Don't let him catch your eye.'

'I don't think he'll come after me today,' I said. 'The girl in the picture is ready for him but I'm not.'

'He's the one who decides who's ready,' said Adam. When we were outside in the twilight he sang me the Schubert song 'Death and the Maiden', 'Der Tod und das Mädchen'. 'Pass by, ah! pass by, go, wild boneman!' says the girl. 'I am still young, go, dear, and do not touch me.' His natural voice was a baritone but he sang the girl's words in such a way that it raised the hairs on the back of my neck. She was so young, so scared, so desperate to live! Death was nothing to the stone sphinxes but they seemed to be paying close attention in the twilight.

'*Das Mädchen* isn't ready to go,' said Adam, but *der Tod* has heard all that before and he means to have his way with her. 'Give me your hand, you fair and tender creature,' he says. 'I am a friend and come not to punish. Be of good courage! I am not wild, you will

28

be sleeping gently in my arms.' He sang the Death part in a very low voice, very measured – it was like the tolling of a bell made of shadows.

It was getting colder as the sky grew dark and the lights below us made me feel colder still as we walked down the Lower Belvedere. We went on to Zu den Drei Hacken in the Stephansdom Quarter for Wiener schnitzel and beer and *Marillenschnaps*, then we walked to the borrowed flat where Adam was staying. I looked up at the sky and found the Plough and the North Star; as long as I can do that I feel at home wherever I am.

I like being in strangers' places. The furniture was old and brown and highly varnished, there were a lot of books, there was a framed photograph of Louise Brooks as Lulu, there was a lamp with a red shade on the bedside table and through the windows I could see the spires of the cathedral. I was excited and nervous – I was afraid that at any moment the scene would freeze like a photograph and be taken away from me. I wanted us to be naked and safe in each other's arms.

Adam lit a stick of sandalwood incense and stuck it in the top of a miniature skull, then he put on a Django Reinhardt LP. 'Nuages' was one of the tracks and we drifted with it and had more *Marillenschnaps*. The red-shaded lamp made a pinky glow while we took out clothes off. Adam was lean and muscular with a sharp hawk-like face, he looked as if he was made for climbing mountains and maybe falling off them. His nakedness made my heart go out to him. The

29

music was actually saying things that words couldn't although I did say, 'Am I better than a sphinx?' and Adam said, 'You're better than anything.' People speak of 'making love' when they talk about the sexual act. Sometimes it is and sometimes it isn't. This time I thought it was. When we finally rolled apart and lay there catching our breath he said, 'Trees are dangerous, you know.'

I said, 'Actually, I haven't had any trouble with them so far.'

'You've heard of the *Erlkonig*, the Erlking?'

'No.'

'His name means Alderking but he hangs out in birches also. He goes where he wants.'

'So what about him? What's his thing?'

'He and his daughters, they make people dead.'

'Right. I'm not around alders or birches very much but I'll be careful. Thanks for the tip.'

'My grandfather was photographing birches on the Teufelsmoor, the Devil's Moor near Worpswede one Christmas. He was found dead among those trees.'

'What killed him?'

'What do you think?'

'Tell me.'

'I'll sing you a song.' He climbed out of bed naked, picked up a guitar, and sang 'Herr Oluf' and translated it for me. 'Nobody is safe anywhere, really,' he said.

'I feel safe being unsafe with you,' I said. 'Come back to bed.' He did and we made love some more and fell asleep and I dreamt that Death stepped out of the Egon Schiele painting and made a pass at me.

When I got back to the Inter-Continental next morning I was told that Sid was dead. He'd jumped off the tenth-storey balcony some time during the night. He'd stuck a note to the balcony railing: 'I'm catching a ride with Anubis.' I hadn't had any kind of premonition or whatever it is that I sometimes get. The last time I saw him he didn't look like a photograph. Maybe I should have felt guilty about going off with Adam but I didn't.

We still had the gig to do. Jimmy Wicks and I took over the songs that Sid would have done. When I saw Adam that evening I felt that I'd made a choice but I didn't want to push it. If he'd asked me to drop everything and go away with him I'd have done it. I gave him my address and telephone number in London. 'Give me yours,' I said, 'so we can stay in touch.'

'I don't think that would be a good idea,' he said. 'My wife is very jealous.'

'Your wife,' I said.

'She doesn't mind what I do when I'm touring,' he said, 'but she doesn't like it when I get phone calls at home.' I looked at him and yes, he was like a photograph.

I was thinking about that when Elias brought me back to the present. 'Can you sing "Herr Oluf" in German?' he said.

'OK,' I said, 'just the first verse:'

Herr Oluf reitet spat und weit
zu bieten auf seine Hochzeitleut.

Herr Oluf rides late and far
to invite guests to his wedding.

Da tanzten die Elfen auf grunem Sand,
Erlkonigs Tochter reicht ihm die Hand.

There dance the elves on a green bank,
the Erlking's daughter reaches out her hand to him.

Wilkommen, Herr Oluf, komm tanze mit mir,
zwei goldene sporen schenke ich dir.

Welcome, Herr Oluf, come dance with me,
two golden spurs I give you.

Elias answered for Herr Oluf:

Ich darf nicht tanzen, nicht tanzen ich mag,
denn morgen ist mein Hochzeittag.'

I may not dance, I don't want to dance,
tomorrow is my wedding day.

'Your voice . . .' he said.
  'My voice what?'
  'It's like my mother's. I could see the alders and the

birches, I could hear the hoof-beats splashing through the swamp.'

I didn't say anything. Hearing that song come out of me had been strange. And the dead man his mother had found among the trees had undoubtedly been Adam's grandfather.

'I'm thinking about how we met,' said Elias. 'How is it that you're a patron of the Royal Academy?'

'Goth rock isn't a for ever thing, Elias, and the people who do it don't always stay the same year after year. Sometimes they change.'

'Maybe their luck changes too.'

'Why'd you say that?'

'I don't know, the words just came out of my mouth.'

I looked at my watch. 'I have a rehearsal to get to.'

'Can I come along?'

I looked at him. Sixty-two but a little like a schoolboy asking for a date. 'OK,' I said. 'The sooner we get through it, the sooner we get through it.'

'Through what, the rehearsal?'

'Not that – *this*.'

'And what would you say this is?'

'A mistake, probably. Let's go.'

4

ANNELIESE NEWMAN

22 January 2003. So. Now I have ninety-two years, that is how it is. The years lie one on top of another like a wobbly stack of plates. All of these plates have on them life-pictures and thought-pictures amd on the topmost plate I sit. When the stack topples, down I come and I am dead. The plates are all shattered, the pictures scattered in little sharp-edged pieces. Where will those little pieces go when I am dead? Maybe to people who are not dead; they will find pictures and bits of pictures in their heads and they won't know what they mean, any more than I do with some of the little pieces in my head. Look, here is the moon, here are mountains, here is the sea, here are two sphinxes.

Why did I like to sing 'Herr Oluf' to my son? I think much about the Erlking's daughter, how she appears not always the same, is not always to be recognised. I thought he might hear not in the words but in my voice that the Erlking's daughter is what pulls you away from where you thought to go. From where it seemed you were meant to go. And maybe you want to go with her, maybe she brings you not to Death but to something new. Maybe if Herr Oluf had gone with her he would not have ridden home dead. Sometimes I talk nonsense, this comes of living too much alone.

That man I ran away with, that tenor. Schlange, Schinken, Schwenk. Peter Schwenk. Maybe now he is dead, not everyone lives so long as I. *Die Entführung aus dem Serail*, he was Belmonte in the Susquehanna Opera production and he promised me I should one day be Constanze but I never rose above 'Turkish woman'. Not a good man, really, not a nice man but I left my husband and my children and went with him. Now I am here in this place that stinks of old women and I have little pieces of pictures in my head, yes? What is the world but little pieces of pictures and who can see a whole one?

5

ELIAS NEWMAN

22 January 2003. The whole time we were in the taxi we didn't talk much, and when we did it was only to point out this or that or comment on what we were passing. I still wanted to know about her reaction to *The Cyclops* but I never found a way to ask, because even as little as I knew Christabel I sensed that a wrong word could bring the shutters down.

From time to time I've tried my hand at poetry. Some years ago I published a little collection with Obelisk. *Litanies and Laments* was the title, and the name I used was Rodney Spoor. I think they printed fifty copies, of which eight or nine were sold and the rest remaindered. Fortunately I hadn't quit my day job. I have a reason for mentioning this which will shortly be apparent.

The strangeness of being with Christabel Alderton was brought home to me geographically in our expedition to the rehearsal studio in Bermondsey. In all the years I'd lived in London I'd never ventured into that part of it but I was heartened to see that the taxi did not fall off the edge of the world. There were glimpses of Waterloo Station and the London Eye, a few brief accelerations, many standstills and one or two U-turns. Signs indicated London Bridge but in time we achieved Jamaica Road and turned off into St James Road. Clements Road appeared and open gates, beyond which stood a tall directory of what was on offer at the Tower Bridge Business Complex.

'We want Building D,' said Christabel to our driver. We were then drawn into an anonymity of large brick warehouse-looking buildings with giant yellow letters distinguishing one from another. London as I knew it seemed far away.

'Doesn't seem very musical around here,' I said.

'Atmosphere is for tourists,' said Christabel. 'This is where the real thing gets put together. You've heard of Duran Duran?'

'I've seen the name. Are they the real thing?'

'They rehearse here. George Michael?'

'Didn't he die?'

'That was Freddie Mercury.'

'Right. George Michael is the one who was had up for cottaging, yes?'

'Yes. He rehearses here too.'

'What does he rehearse?'

'You're pulling my leg.'

'Not on the first date.'

'This isn't a date, remember?' We were now at Building D. 'Waterloo Sunset Studios are in here.'

We were admitted by a pretty young woman called Claire who was wearing a beige jumper and black silky-looking trousers. As she led the way to the lift I was thinking that Mobile Mortuary might be more of a class act than I'd assumed.

'I'm reading your mind,' said Christabel.

'Musical thoughts,' I said.

'Ben's booked you into the new South Studio,' said Claire as she slid the heavy metal door shut.

'Who's Ben?' I asked Christabel.

'Ben Saltzman. He's our production manager. He makes everything happen. He books our flights and we fly to wherever it says on the tickets. Or a bus pulls up and we jump in. All we have to do is make music or whatever it is that we do when we get there.'

'I wish a bus would pull up for me to jump into. Or a plane.'

'And what would you do when you got to wherever it was going?'

'I'd work that out when I got there.'

The freight lift smelled of old iron and machine oil and I expected the South Studio to smell of old flooring and radiators that knocked as they got too hot. With fluorescent lighting that buzzed and flickered. But when we came out of the lift everything we saw was new and bright. We passed several studios, from one of which issued a volume of noise that I could feel from the soles of my feet to the top of my head. 'What in the world is that?' I said.

'Unholy Din,' said Claire.

'I noticed, but what band is it?'

'Unholy Din is the name of the band,' said Christabel.

The South Studio was full of clear grey winter daylight. The new grey carpet and the dark-blue fabric walls had no smell at all, only an air of waiting for things to happen. There were black oblongs as big as doors suspended from the high ceiling. Other black shapes like giant frogs crouched on the floor. 'What are those?' I asked Christabel.

'The overhead things are sound deflectors – they focus it and keep it from bouncing all over the place.'

'And the giant frogs?'

'Monitor wedges. So we can hear what we're doing.'

'And what about the electrified steamer trunks?'

'Speakers, amps – we're only using one cabinet each.'

'What's in the cabinets?' I said, thinking of drinks.

'Speakers,' said Christabel.

'If you're not already famous, you could *get* famous,' said the giant frogs, and suddenly I wished I were young, and good with a guitar.

Looking around at the studio and the equipment I was impressed by the logistics of rock and said so to Christabel.

'You've no idea,' she said. 'Here's Ben with a couple of kilos of paperwork.' She introduced us, then said to Ben, 'If you've got a moment, show Elias some of what you're doing.'

Ben was a not very big man who looked as if he might do bare-knuckle fighting in his spare time. He came up to scratch, fixed me with a beady eye, and said, 'Ever seen a production rider?'

'No,' I said, 'I haven't.'

He led with a wodge of printed pages. 'See if you can guess what's in here.'

'Well, it would have to be production details, yes? Transport, catering, scheduling and so forth?'

'Have a look.' His roundhouse right was a contract between THE ARTISTE [Mobile Mortuary] and THE MANAGEMENT [Maccabee Enterprises]. It started with percentages and payments and other money matters including MARKETING. Then came PRODUCTION RE-QUIREMENTS beginning with STAGE SIZE and SOUND WINGS, STAGE CONSTRUCTION, STAIRS, LOADING RAMPS, POWER REQUIREMENTS FOR LIGHTING, FOR SOUND, moving on to MAIN DRESSING ROOM, TUNE-UP ROOM etc. but soon arriving at HOT COOKED ENGLISH-TYPE BREAKFAST PLUS CEREALS, TOAST & JAMS × 10, progressing through LUNCH × 10 and DINNER × 17 to the dressing rooms and 8 × BOTTLES OF GOOD WINE 4 × RED 4 × WHITE (NOT CHARDONNAY), 12 X BOTTLES OF GOOD BEER, 12 × CANS OF DIET COKE, 12 × LARGE BOTTLES OF STILL WATER, 12 × SMALL BOTTLES OF STILL WATER, 2 × LARGE BOTTLES OF PERRIER WATER, thence onward with 1 × KETTLE AND COFFEE MACHINE, BISCUITS, BANANAS, KIWI FRUIT, STRAWBERRIES, ETC., SELEC-

TION OF CHOCOLATE INC. KIT KAT, more drinks 1 HOUR PRIOR TO SHOW TIME and 30 MINS PRIOR TO SHOW TIME and BAND BUS AFTER SHOW. There was a great deal more of this on the production rider, and while my mind was still boggling and gurgling with it, Ben, who already had me in chancery, delivered a facer with more sheets of paper including the equipment freight list, diagrams of the band setup on stage, input channels and microphone lists, the light rig and theatre lighting, all with recondite nomenclature and endless specifications.

'More to it than you thought?' said Ben, graciously stepping back.

'Definitely,' I said. 'I don't know how you keep track of it all.'

'Years of experience,' he said, and retired to his office.

In a mentally flattened state I was led carefully over cables and around large objects to be introduced to Christabel's colleagues: Jimmy Wicks and Howard Dent, guitars; Bert Gresham, bass; Buck Travis, keyboards; Shorty Strong, drums. Jimmy had a grandfatherly paunch and was mostly bald but with a ponytail; watching his right elbow and wrist when he checked his guitar I could see that he suffered from repetitive strain injury; Howard was presenting with what I've heard described as the Hendrix hunch as well as RSI; Bert had some kind of tic; and from the way Shorty cupped his ear when they were talking I assumed that his hearing was impaired.

Christabel followed my glance and shrugged. 'But we're famous,' she said.

When the band were ready to work they went into a huddle. They stayed that way without saying anything for about a minute, then the huddle broke up and the band took up their instruments and produced various levels of feedback. Christabel sat down with me while they noodled around with sundry riffs. 'Every tour it takes longer for them to get their chops together,' she said.

'Chops?'

'Their technical and physical fitness, their Make-It-Happen.'

'What was the huddle for?' I asked her.

'We always have a moment with Anubis before we start work.'

'Anubis!'

'The Egyptian jackal-headed god who conducts your soul from this world to the next.'

'I know who Anubis is, but how come Mobile Mortuary huddle with him?'

Christabel told me about Sid Horstmann's suicide and the note he left. 'We don't know where he is now,' she said, 'so in the huddle we give Anubis the latest news and our love to pass along to Sid.'

'His suicide must still be with you. What an awful thing!'

'Please! People always feel they have to say something when there's nothing to say.'

'Sorry. Do you really believe in Anubis?'

'I believe in everything and nothing. Anubis is a way of focusing our Sid thoughts. Am I too crazy for you?'

'Not at all, I'm catching up fast.'

'Let's do "Gypsy Me, Django" from the top,' said Jimmy as he and Christabel stepped up to the microphones. The band started very quietly with a slant version of 'Two Guitars' that made my throat ache. The music faded to a whisper behind Jimmy's guitar as he sang:

Django, gypsy on the edge of night,
Long time gone on roads nobody knows, . . .

'Stop,' said Jimmy, 'I want to try it with that new riff I worked out yesterday.' They fussed over that for a while, then Jimmy started again:

Django, gypsy on the edge of night,
Long time gone on roads nobody knows,
Gone with the singing where the fires burned bright,
Gone in the silence where the music goes.

Christabel came in with:

Gypsy me with you on your road so far,
Gypsy me fires on the edge of night,
Gypsy me under your wandering star,
Gypsy me Django burning bright.

She was looking right at me so she couldn't miss the

expression on my face. She was singing words that I'd written. Her voice was like breath on a mirror; it came and went with misty transience out of two big flat speakers that stood on legs and were only for the vocal. The way she sang gave me goose pimples and she herself seemed much affected by the song. She was quiet then while the band took over for a bit, then she and Jimmy came in together with:

Django, gypsy on the edge of night,
Django, Django burning bright.

They went through it again, elaborating on it the second time round; they used repetitions, they extended some lines and broke up others in strange ways but it was my poem, 'Lament for Django', living a strange new life with Mobile Mortuary. Hearing it come back to me in this incarnation was unsettling. They worked in quotes from *Dies Irae* and 'California Dreaming' in uneasy rhythms and odd intervals and it was unlike any musical experience I'd had before. When they finished they paused to fiddle with the new riff and argue technicalities.

I said to Christabel, 'Did you set that poem to music?'

'Yes. How'd you know it was a poem?'

'It's called "Lament for Django" and I wrote it.'

'No you didn't, it was written by Rodney Spoor.'

'That's me. I'm Rodney Spoor.'

'I don't believe it.'

'"Lament for Django" was in a 1978 collection, *Litanies and Laments*, that I wrote under the name of Rodney Spoor.'

'Jesus!' said Christabel. 'A poet! And I thought you were a perfectly respectable guy.'

'I'm a doctor as I told you. When I wrote those poems I thought it would be a good idea to keep my literary life separate from my medical career. There hasn't been any literary life since then so I might just as well not have bothered.'

'I tried to get permission from your publisher,' she said, 'but they've gone out of business.'

'Never mind that. What interests me is that you're singing my words and something brought us together.'

'Maybe. But let's not talk about it.'

'Why not?'

'I'm superstitious.'

'OK. We'll talk about Django.'

'Django!'

'I'm not surprised that you like him. There's a lot of you in his music.'

'Really?'

'"Nuages", for example. If he had known you he might have written that as a musical portrait of you.'

'Of me!' She had her head tilted to one side and was looking at me the way you look at someone when you think they might be getting at you.

'Yes, of you.'

'That's a very nice compliment.' Observing me narrowly. Not an easy woman to compliment.

'I'm a very nice man, actually. Would you have dinner with me this evening?'

'Why not?' she said. 'No reason to stop now.'

From the beginning of the rehearsal one of the crew had been busy at a bank of technology that looked able to handle the *Ark Royal*. 'I've got that one on DAT,' he said. 'Do you want to hear it back?'

'Later,' said Jimmy. To Christabel he said, 'Whenever you can spare the time we'll do "Did It Wasn't?"'

'Remember your blood pressure,' said Christabel. 'I'm ready now.' To me she said, 'This is a new song, all my own words wrote by me.'

The band did a very spooky intro and then Christabel came in with:

Did it wasn't, did it was?
Did I walking in the wasn't, did you
running in the was?
Did you always, did you never?
Did it sometimes, was I clever?
Was it didn't going to wasn't be whatever?
Am I fuzzy, is there fuzz?
Did it wasn't, did it was?

The words passed through themselves and seemed to take the present through the past and back again: Christabel's past and mine, spiralled like a double helix. Why was I still single? For one thing, I never wanted to be in a position where a woman could leave me and wreck my life. My mother had been, as far as I could see, a perfect wife. She and my father seemed happy together, they looked at each other with loving looks. Then all of a sudden, with no warning at all, she was gone. Well, life isn't fair, is it. We all know that and I'm not blaming my woman problems on my mother.

As a bachelor I've never lacked for companionship when I wanted it. Have I ever been in love? I don't think so. There's a chasm between men and women, and love is the rope you fling across. If the other person catches it you have the beginning of a suspension bridge. My rope always fell short. There have been serious girlfriends. The last one, when I was forty-four, was Nikki. She was twenty-seven, clever, had a great sense of humour, and was a stunner. Five foot eleven with a face of commanding beauty, blue eyes, and long dark hair. Better-looking than most models because she had lovely round arms and legs instead of sticks. I'm six foot one and considered not too ugly, so we made the kind of couple people turned to look at. She spoke French, German, Russian and Arabic and she worked in the Ministry of Defence. When I asked her what she did there she laughed and said, 'If I tell you I'll have to kill you.' She said it as a joke but I didn't ask again. I was of course proud to be seen with her and every man who saw us envied me. But it was a terrible strain, I was never convinced that I could hold on to her, and eventually I broke it off before she could dump me. What a relief. Was I in love with her? I guess she was more of a serious acquisition.

By the time I was in my fifties I was too set in my ways and too sunk in my work to look for a wife. Anyhow that's what I told myself.

There's a bronze nude on the Embankment by the Albert Bridge, just standing there thinking her thoughts. Her face turned to the river. I call her Daphne. I used to go jogging on the Embankment and I always patted her bottom as I went by. A limited relationship.

When Christabel finished the song, she and the others talked about the intro and the ending, then the band went into the instrumental bits of other numbers that needed work. Some of the titles were 'Birdshit on Your Statue', 'No More World', 'E-mails from Aliens', and 'Don't Upper My Downer'. While the others tinkered with those and talked technical talk Christabel sat down with me.

'Your song took me to places I haven't been for a while,' I said.

'Did you find your way back?'

'I don't know. I'm here and I'm there.'

'But right now you're at Waterloo Sunset. How come you're a diabetes consultant at a London hospital?

I listened to myself giving her the short version while I mentally reviewed the longer one. I was born in Lansdale, Pennsylvania, where my father had a print shop with a sideline in novelties and business gifts. When my mother ran off with the tenor my two older sisters shouldered the housewifely duties and I helped with various chores. After a year or so my father took up with another woman but soon after that he was diagnosed as having diabetes meilitus and was put on insulin. Next came gall bladder surgery, then his first heart attack. He died three years later, when I was sixteen. He left us well provided for. I'd already decided to become a doctor. I went to Temple University, then Harvard Medical School. I was beginning to wonder about disease as metaphor. Had my father been unable to metabolise the sweetness his new woman gave him? Did the bitterness in him turn to stone? And did he take it all to heart and leave his body with nothing to say except goodbye?

When I qualified I decided to put the past behind me and I hoped the future was in front of me. I wasn't sure where I wanted to be but I thought elsewhere might be good. About that time I had a postcard from London from a school friend I rarely saw. The picture was a 14 bus and the message was: 'This is a great place to feel strange.' So I went to have a look at London. I came for two weeks, decided to live here for a time, registered as an alien, and showed the Home Office that I would not be a burden on the state.

When I decided to stay my qualifications were accepted. This was thirty years ago, so I was not required to sit any examinations. It was a time when England needed specialists and I had an offer from St Eustace. Now at sixty-two I'm a well-established consultant. I do four to five specialist clinics a week and two in-patient ward rounds. The rest of my time is taken up with teaching, research, admin sessions, and my regular stint as specialist in charge of incoming emergency medicine.

'You've done all right with what to be and where to be,' said Christabel. 'Have you worked out *how* to be?'

'Not yet,' I said.

'Let me know when you do.' She said this without cynicism, as if she thought I might come up with an answer that had escaped her. The band was ready for her again and she went back to work.

6

JIMMY WICKS

22 January 2003. You work with somebody for years, you go on tour together, you eat and sleep and go to the toilet in the same bus day after day, mile after mile, you get to know each other's smells but you don't know fuck all. She talks to me about the music, we work on songs together. Does she think there's anything else in my head besides a fuzz box and a wah-wah pedal? She'd probably be surprised to know that I have pictures in my mind apart from what I see with my eyes. Pictures of her sometimes. Strange ones. Naked in a high place. Or looking at me through trees. Like dream pictures with sounds and smells. Sometimes the sea.

How did I get to be what I am, where I am? Nothing unusual about the start of it. Back in the sixties if you wanted to pull the birds you learned how to play a guitar, just like now. And if you couldn't join a band you formed one, so that's what Sid Horstmann and I did. We found two other guys for bass and drums and we put together a kind of skiffle band, The Winkle-Pickers. Learned 'Cumberland Gap' and after a while we got hold of a bloke with a Vox Continental and we were on our way. Did our first gig at The Cave in Bethnal Green and from then on we went up and down and sideways with changes until Buck Travis came in on keyboards in 1972 and Bert and Shorty joined us shortly after. We called ourselves Ouija Board for the first three years, then we changed our act and became Mobile Mortuary. Christabel didn't come into the band until 1980, and that's when we had our first chart record: 'Haunt Me' at No. 3. Thirty-one years this band's been together! A lot of marriages don't last that long.

Sid always had to be the alpha male. He didn't look like James Dean but he tried for a James Dean look. Live fast, die young, and get as much pussy as you can. He wasn't in love with Christabel but he didn't like it when she went out with that weirdo from Sayings of Confucius. She didn't love Sid but she was the one who started this Anubis huddle shit after he was in a body drawer he couldn't climb out of. By now she's so used to feeling guilty she'd be miserable without it. She's fifty-four and I'm sixty. This new boyfriend looks at least as old as I am. I've never made a move yet, each time I thought I might the time didn't seem right. I don't know whether to laugh or cry when I think of how I took up the guitar to pull the birds. Tracy was one of the first I pulled and no sooner had I played a few riffs than she got pregnant. With two big brothers and a father with a very short fuse. Hello, Mrs Jimmy.

After Tracy took the kids and left me I thought I'd come out and tell Christabel how I felt. I didn't, though. She still looks pretty good. I don't know, if I'm careful maybe I can outlive the competition. Time will tell, they say. It's been telling me for years but I try not to listen.

7

CHRISTABEL ALDERTON

22 January 2003. When I got back from Vienna after Sid's death, Victor, one of my cat-minding neighbours, gave me a recording of 'Songs of the Humpback Whale'. He hadn't yet heard about Sid, he just gave it to me because he thought I might like it. 'It's deep,' he said. When I played it, it was as if the whales and the sea were singing my thoughts and singing the dead. Sometimes Death himself would sing in a very low-frequency whale voice, grunting and growling, and the whale voice of me would plead with him, weeping and wailing in higher frequencies. And all the time the watery deep-sea voices were burbling and plashing all around. After that first hearing I didn't want to listen to it again for a long time but every once in a while it was the only thing I listened to. Now after all these years I hear it in my head without playing the CD.

I didn't want this dinner date to be too serious and I had a craving for fish and chips so Elias suggested The White Horse in Parson's Green. 'They do cod in beer batter,' he said. 'I think you'll like it.' By the time the rehearsal was over it was almost eight so we took a taxi straight there. On the way we talked a little about music. Classical is what he listens to mostly, he said Haydn quartets would be his Desert Island Discs. He remembered people headbanging to Hawkwind and Status Quo and he liked The Rolling Stones, also Portishead and Garbage but that was about it for rock and pop, he'd never heard of Joe Strummer. He likes blues and Thelonious Monk, he likes country and western and he knows a lot of standards but I wasn't sure how we were going to get through the evening until we started talking about painters. He's a big Redon user and he has a thing for Caspar David Friedrich. I have a tattoo of a Friedrich owl, wings outspread, perched on a grave marker just above my bottom cleavage. Not many people know that.

The White Horse seemed to be popular with Hooray Henrys and Henriettas. Even on this cold January evening they were stood three deep outside the pub and clogging the entrance, none of them over thirty and all of them loud. 'There's a dining room at the back,' said Elias. 'It's fairly quiet there.' We struggled through the braying and the cigarette smoke, reached the dining room and sat down at a table for two. The other tables were braying less loudly than the people in the bar. There were some crap abstractions on the walls doing some visual braying but they went quiet when I looked away. We ordered the beer-battered cod and pints of Bass and there we were then, at the point where one of the two people says, 'So . . .' This time I said it, 'So . . . Here we are. What now?'

'Why do you sound so negative, as if nothing good can happen?' said Elias.

Tell me about negative, I thought. My son Django was four when I took him to Maui with me. It was January, the band had nothing scheduled for a couple of weeks and I wanted to see those humpback whales that come there every year. I'd been having dreams in which I was drowning in the sea while the whales sang all around me but I wanted to see them anyhow. Then I dreamt that Django was in the sea, sinking down, down, down into the darkness. When I woke up I thought, he could fall over the side of a boat. So when we got to Maui we didn't go out on a whale-watching boat; instead we watched from a cliff and Django fell off the cliff and was killed. He'd be fourteen now and a good-looking boy. 'Negative?' I said to Elias. 'I guess I'm just that kind of person. Tomorrow you can try someone else.'

'I don't want to try someone else,' he said.

'What are you looking for?' I asked him.

'What am I looking for?'

'Don't answer a question by repeating it. What are you looking for with me?'

'I hadn't thought it out, Christabel. You started it with that line from "Herr Oluf"; I'm just going from one moment to the next with you and I'll go as far as it goes.'

'Brave words. Have you got a video of *Vertigo*?'

'Yes, I have.'

'Good. After we get out of here let's go to your place and watch it.'

'OK, we'll do that. Any reason for that particular film?'

'Not really, I just feel like watching it with you.' We talked some more about Friedrich and Böcklin and Bresdin, had two more pints and coffee, then we left The White Horse and walked to Elias's place on the other side of Eelbrook Common. Here I was in another January ten years after the one when I lost Django. January weather suits my January mood. I like it when the days are cold and grey and rainy and the nights are early and dark and huddly. The lights on the New King's Road and on both sides of the common made it seem darker where we were and now it started to rain. Again there was an invisible helicopter near and far, near and far. Behind us the District Line trains rumbled and clacked as shadowy people passed us coming and going on the shining paved paths. Sometimes, I was thinking, everywhere is nowhere and nowhere isn't a bad place to be.

Elias's house was enormous, four storeys with a roof extension. 'Do you live all by yourself in this whole place?' I asked him.

'Yes,' he said. 'I'm used to being alone with a lot of space around me. And I'm a big accumulator – books, recordings, videos.'

We got out of our wet coats and towelled our heads dry, then we settled down in the ground floor living room and Elias got us some cognac and lit a fire in the fireplace. By now the rain was drumming on the windows and there was a lot of bleak midwinter going on outside but it was big-time cosy where we were. There were shelves full of books catching gleams from the fire, and china and bronze figures taking the shadows and the light. I had the feeling that Elias's house didn't look empty when nobody was in it. 'Here's to whatever,' I said as we clinked glasses.

'I'll drink to that,' he said.

'Roll on *Vertigo*,' I said. 'Let's get suspenseful.'

'But you *have* seen it?' he said. 'You know how it ends?'

'Sure, but each time I see it I hope the end will be different.'

'So you're a positive thinker after all.'

'In a negative way. Are you ready in the projection booth?'

As there may still be one or two people out there who've not seen *Vertigo*, I won't disclose any more of the plot than I have to. James Stewart plays an ex-cop who had to leave the force because after a disastrous rooftop chase he has a fear of heights and gets dizzy when high up. Knowing this, an old friend hires Stewart to shadow his wife because he says he's afraid she's suicidal. This is a hoax that draws Stewart into an elaborate murder plot. Kim Novak is part of it but she and Stewart fall in love with each other, which was not in the plan. When he finds out much later how he's been duped he becomes bitter and cynical.

I've given a lot of thought to the Kim Novak character. She's got a shady past, she's definitely a bad-luck woman but she's touching and vulnerable and beautiful and she's never stopped loving Stewart. Does she deserve a second chance?

'There are holes in that plot you could drive a truck through,' said Elias.

'I know that,' I said, 'but what about the Kim Novak character? If you were in Stewart's place, would you make her climb the stairs in the old mission?'

'No, I wouldn't.'

'Are you sure? After all, anything with her was going to end up badly one way or another – she was definitely unlucky.'

'How could I reject her? I fell in love with her because of her self, regardless of her part in the hoax. There was a strangeness about her, she seemed a prisoner locked in the mystery of herself – only love could free her and I was still in love with her, never mind how I'd been used, I wouldn't care about that. Love isn't a rational thing. I'd never have made her climb those stairs, never.'

'That's a very passionate speech. Have you ever been in love, Elias?'

'Not like that, not irrationally.'

'Pour some more cognac,' I said, 'and let's look at the shapes in the fire.'

8

ELIAS NEWMAN

23 January 2003. An owl tattoo. Not just any old owl but a beautifully-done copy of a Caspar David Friedrich owl, wings outspread, perched on the little roof of a wooden-cross grave marker. This is the bird I know as a great horned owl; in German it's called *uhu*. Spreading its wings across her sacrum. Without thinking I said, 'Who's buried there?'

'Various hopes,' she said, and began to cry. I took her in my arms and she was shaking all over. I got her into bed and under the duvet and held her while she cried herself out. I felt a fool for saying what I had and I was honoured that she was giving me her naked sobbing. What was she crying about? I wondered. Anything to do with that owl tattoo? What buried hopes did it signify? And it wasn't like a photograph or a note you can tear up and throw away; it was permanent, following her around for ever.

When her sobbing had died down to whimpers and sniffles she sighed and cuddled closer and fell asleep in my arms. After a while I gently withdrew the arm she was lying on and I fell asleep too. That was the extent of our lovemaking on our first night together.

In the morning she woke up with a smile, hugged me, looked at her watch, and said, 'I've got a recording session.' She and her owl flew out of bed and into the bathroom, from where she emerged fully dressed in about half a minute.

'I'll make us some breakfast,' I said.

'No time,' she said. 'Phone you later.' She blew me a kiss and was off down the stairs and away, leaving only the smell of her in my bed. Not a fragrance out of a bottle but her own smell that had in it her nakedness against mine. Not a word about the owl tattoo.

I was still trying to figure out our *Vertigo* session. It had been some kind of test and I'd passed but I didn't know why. The Kim Novak character was called Madeleine Elster. Christabel obviously identified strongly with her but again I didn't know why. Madeleine Elster was unlucky, she'd said. Anything with her was going to end up badly. Was Christabel speaking about herself? She was surrounding herself with a hedge of mysteries and warnings, becoming, intentionally or not, a fairy-tale princess. Naturally I was beginning to feel like the prince who would break through that hedge to rescue her. Had I ever been in love, she wanted to know. Not irrationally, I'd said. But what other way was there to be in love? And was I?

It was Thursday, a working day for me. I thought she might have been a little more forthcoming than that speedy hug and kiss. I didn't need a certificate of my sensitivity and understanding but there could have been more of . . . I don't know. On the other hand, maybe the easy ordinariness of her departure was her way of showing that there was more between us than there'd been before. Yes, I was back at the high-school level of wondering about girls. Would she go to the prom with me? Mustn't rush things. I sighed and caught an 11 bus to St Eustace.

It's an old hospital and it smells old. The flickering fluorescent lighting made the day seem as wintry indoors as out. I took the lift to the third floor and got ready to stick my thumb in the dyke yet again while the flood of diabetes rose higher and the walking statistics briefly abandoned McDonald's and Pizza Hut and Coca-Cola to present themselves to me. There are of course more young ones than there used to be but most of them are middle-aged or older, some walking unaided, others with sticks or in wheelchairs, all of them unable to metabolise the satisfaction they're greedy for. As far as I know there is no Sweetaholics Anonymous. And along with their burgers and fries the diabetics are eating up more NHS money all the time. Right now we're spending ten per cent of our £72 million budget on treating the disease; by 2010 it'll be twenty per cent. Things change, but always, it seems, for the worse.

I do what I can and console myself with small gains:

Imran Patel has been balancing his blood sugar better than he did six months ago; Sarah Blum's Charcot joint has reached Stage 4 and she's ready for a surgical boot, and so on. In the meantime I continue my research on the aetiology of the disease and the psychology of diabetics.

While I was working my way through the morning a motorbike messenger arrived with a ticket for the Mobile Mortuary concert at the Hammersmith Apollo on Friday. There was also a pass for the hospitality suite after the concert, and a note that said, '*Can't see you till after the gig. XXX*' Three paper kisses. Could do better. Humming 'Is That All There Is' I went through folders, checked histories, sent people for blood tests and X-rays and various scans, and in between ran my eye over the proofs for the third edition of *Lipids: An Overview*, a pocket picture guide on which I collaborated with the biochemist Phil Winston. This little book is elegantly produced; the tables and diagrams inspire the hope that there are answers for almost everything, while the photographs of such things as tuberous xanthomas and diabetic gangrene make it clear that for many the answers come too late. Between the clarity of the physician and the confusion of the afflicted the gap is wide and on some days I think it will never be narrowed.

Of course I didn't stop thinking about Christabel. While doing that I had a mental visit from Professor Ernst, my predecessor, who walked into my mind without knocking and shook his head. 'It's a matter of the vertical *vis-à-vis* the horizontal,' he once told me. He wore a pince-nez that never fell off. 'The doctor is vertical; the patient is horizontal, even when they're walking around. The doctor wears a suit, the patient is in pyjamas, even when they're fully dressed. Keep this distinction in mind because a lot of people who aren't patients should be patients of one kind or another if you take my meaning. Also: don't sleep with anyone who doesn't play golf.' I don't know why I was remembering his advice now. I was his registrar at the clinic for the ten years before his retirement. I doubt that Christabel plays golf. I've never slept with anyone who did.

When was I first attracted to Christabel? It was when I saw her standing in front of *The Cyclops*. She wasn't just looking at the painting, she was giving herself to it, and as I've said before, her response excited me. Then when she smiled I wondered what she was smiling about.

Now in my working day I remembered her trembling last night and my right arm involuntarily moved to encircle her.

9

TITUS SMART

23 January 2003. I've been Elias Newman's registrar for five years. What with his research and his writing in addition to the hospital work he's the busiest man I know. Whenever I come into his office he's fully engaged with one thing or another. But today he was just standing by the window, apparently lost in thought. He turned to me and said, 'Yes?' With some impatience, I felt.

'Never mind,' I said. 'It can wait.'

'Right,' he said, and went back to his thoughts. Most unusual.

10

CHRISTABEL ALDERTON

23 January 2003. OK, the owl tattoo. I get so tired
of explaining everything, even to myself. When I
got back from Maui in 1993 I wanted to, I don't
know, draw a line under that time? Put it all behind
me? That sounds like a joke in view of where the
tattoo ended up. I've said before that I do a lot of
stupid things, right? So I had this book my neigh-
bour Victor had given me and in it were some Caspar
David Friedrich owls that really talked to me. The
one I decided on, sitting on a grave marker with his
wings outspread, he was like an orchestra conductor,
very much in charge and he was commanding silence.
His whole body was saying, 'OK, that's it.' I got a
photocopy of it and took it to the Fulham Tattoo
Centre. The walls were full of dragons, devils, hearts
and flowers and skeletons and whatnot and there
were a couple of pretty girls discussing body piercing.
One of the signs on the wall said that nobody under
the influence of drink or drugs would be tattooed.

It was a grey day with reality coming down like rain.

'Where do you want this and how big?' said the man. When I told him he looked at me sideways and said, 'You're not on anything, are you?'

'No,' I said. 'Do I look like I am?'

'Kind of.'

'What, you want me to pee in a cup so you can test it?'

'Calm down, OK? It's just that you might not be quite yourself today.'

'How do you know I'm not like this *every* day?'

'Look,' he said, 'once you get this on you it's there for good, so it's best not to do anything you'll be sorry for.'

'All my life I've done things I've been sorry for,' I said. 'Why should I stop now?'

'OK, I'll do this owl for you if that's what you really want. First I have to make a tracing for the transfer. Come back tomorrow and I'll be ready for you. It'll cost you fifty pounds.' So the next day I came back and now that owl is part of me.

I know that I tend to make a mystery of myself with Elias. Well, I have a lot to be mysterious about. I was nineteen when I married Richard Turpin. I was singing with an all-girl group called The Nectarines. That was in 1968. We were doing a gig at the Orford Cellar in Norwich with some of our own songs and a few covers. This bloke who was very close to the stage kept staring as if he'd never seen anything like me before. We wore miniskirts and fringey tops and

I've always had good legs. After the last set he came up to me and said, 'Hi, I'm Dick Turpin.'

'Where's your horse?' I said.

'My horse is a white Ford Transit with a ladder on top,' he said, and gave me his card:

Dick Turpin
The Highway Roofer
'We've got it covered.'

'Great,' I said. 'Next time I need a roof I'll ring you up.'

'I'm putting together a brochure,' he said, 'and I want to feature you in it.'

'Wow,' I said. 'This could be my big break. Does that happen before or after you ask me up to see your roof tiles?'

'Come on, do I look like that kind of guy?'

'Yes.' He looked like Jack the Lad with an indoor complexion even though he did outdoor work. His mouth was smiling but something about his eyes made me wonder if there was a peephole in the dressing-room wall. He was a big man with big strong hands. Like my stepfather who was always opening the door of my room without knocking. He'd managed to catch me in my underwear once or twice but he'd never got further than that. I'd been thinking it was high time I got a new roof over my head.

'What I have in mind,' said Jack the Roofing Lad, 'is a back view of you climbing a ladder in a Dick

Turpin T-shirt and a skirt a little shorter than the one you have on now.'

'Cheeky,' I said. 'Do I get to show my face at all?'

'Of course. When you reach the scaffolding you turn and smile and we'll have a close-up with my message under it: FOR A ROOF YOU CAN LOOK UP TO, PHONE DICK TURPIN FOR A FREE ESTIMATE! There's three hundred quid in it for you.'

So I did it, one thing led to another, and I very quickly got a new roof over my head. Dick got what my stepfather hadn't and it was legal. He was not a gentleman in bed or out of it. He drank a lot of beer and he watched a lot of football, sometimes at our house with men from his crew who also drank a lot of beer, sometimes at other places. The house was nothing wonderful, a small brick end-of-terrace with two up and two down. With a leaky roof that he never got round to fixing. The Nectarines disbanded and there I was being some kind of housewife. It wasn't quite my idea of getting out into the world.

It lasted almost a year and by that time Dick had knocked me about a few times too many with his big strong hands. He went off to work one rainy day when I was wishing he'd fall off a roof. He did and it killed him. My judgement has never been good but neither was his.

I wonder what Elias would think if I stopped being a mystery and told him just how risky it is to get too close to me. Stevo's been OK so far but maybe he has nine lives. When I got back to my house after Django's death I found this tiger-striped kitten in a basket on my doorstep. He looked up at me as if Django's spirit had gone into him. I couldn't give a cat his name so I named him after Stephane Grappelli.

If Elias were smart he'd find somebody safer to get mixed up with.

11

ANNELIESE NEWMAN

24 January 2003. I don't think of my daughters very often. Wherever they are, they have done all right, that I know. Sometimes I think of Elias because there are things I want to tell him. These things he knows maybe, maybe not.

Everything is twice itself, this I often think. Things are what they are every day, but then sometimes they are not. Sometimes I see people talking, crossing the road, running to catch a bus. Suddenly it is like TV with the sound turned off and I see that this is really Death dressing himself up as these people talking, crossing the road, running to catch a bus. So that is what is really happening, no?

But who am I that I should say this? My mind is like a top that spins crazily just before it falls over.

12

ELIAS NEWMAN

24 January 2003. Sometimes I wonder if I am the sort
of person who's really suited to a career in medicine.
My mind is subject to fits of strangeness; this morning
coming to work I looked out of the bus window at
people talking, crossing the road, running to catch the
bus and I thought, all this is really only Death dressing
himself up as people talking, crossing the road, running
to catch the bus. Ought a doctor to see things in that
way? But it's not surprising that Death comes into my
mind; I know quite a few people my age who are
dead, even some younger than I. I do what I do and
I advance in my profession but it could well be too
late for any personal development, any future with a
woman. I'm sure there are people who get all the way
to the end of their lives and die without ever having
been in love. Still, I *do* feel that connection with
Christabel that was there even before we met. Did it
will be?

13

CHRISTABEL ALDERTON

24 January 2003. The cyclops turned up in a dream last night. Staring at me through a clump of trees. Birches, thin scraggley ones. The ground was boggy, squelching under my feet and there was that hideous face gawking at me with its one staring eye and its disgusting little mouth saying something but I couldn't hear what it was. 'What?' I said. 'Are you the Erlking now?' But it just kept moving its mouth and my own voice woke me up.

Adam Freund was Django's father. Although I was sharing a bed with Sid Horstmann we hadn't had sex since my last period and I was ovulating when I was with Adam. The band was back in London two days later and I never saw him again. When I found that I was pregnant I wondered how he'd feel about it if he knew. When we were together in that borrowed room, before he told me he was married, I knew that he was the right man for me. If he'd asked me to drop every-thing and go away with him I'd have done it. But as it was, even if I'd known where to reach him, what would have been the point? I used to lie in bed and grind my teeth thinking about it. If only he weren't married!

Sid Horstmann was wrong for me but I was with him long enough for him to kill himself. Why did I take up with him? Working together and travelling together made it easier of course and he had had a sort of doomed air that attracted me. Did I think I could save him from whatever he was heading for? I know now that you can't save anybody. He had a lot of talent and he wrote some good songs but he had black moods and fits of depression that weren't helped by his drinking. Maybe I helped him over that balcony railing by getting bored with his need for special treatment. It would have been better for both of us if I'd said no the first time he wanted to get a leg over.

My night with Adam was in 1988. In 1990 Mobile Mortuary were back in Vienna and Sayings of Confucius were our support band again. Adam wasn't with them. 'He's dead,' they told me. 'We were in Hamburg setting up for a gig at Onkel Po's Carnegie Hall and the light rig fell on him.' So he wasn't married any more but he wasn't available. When Django was three I told him about it and some time after that he showed me a drawing of a man. It was done the way little kids draw people, a big head with arms and legs growing out of it. Big smile on the man's face and he was holding a guitar.

'Who's that?' I said.

Django said, 'Dad. He played me a song.'

'In a dream?'

'Yes.'

'Do you remember how it went?'

'Yes.'

'Can you hum it?'

So he hummed 'Nuages'. He'd heard me play it often and he had a good ear. Django's coffin was made on Maui by Rudy Ka'uhane, a local craftsman. On the lid he lettered:

O winds, winds of Waipio,
In the calabash of Kaleiioku,
Come from the ipu-makani!
O wind, the wind of Hilo,
Come quickly, come with power!

'This is the kite-flying song of the demigod Maui,' said Rudy. 'Now the soul of your son flies like a kite and the string is in your hand.'

When I got to Honolulu my flight home wasn't due to leave until next morning. In the airport the part of my brain that makes sense of what the eyes see didn't seem to be working, all the colours weren't any colour and the shapes wouldn't stay the same. Hello darkness, I thought, but there wasn't any proper darkness either. I breathed in the ghosts of long-gone burgers and fries and when I went to the ladies' the air freshener smelled like Juicy Fruit. I wasn't hungry but I felt like eating so I had a couple of spring rolls at the Fresh Express cafeteria. There were neon signs in English and Japanese and the spring rolls probably had some flavour but I didn't know what it was.

I spent the night at the Mini Hotel Sleep/Shower in the airport. It was like a cell for a monk, very quiet and away from everything. The bedsteads were iron, the blankets were thin and grey like prison blankets, the towels were only a little thicker than the toilet paper, but that monk's cell of a room kept all the bits of me from flying apart. It held me together until the coffin and I were on the plane. Lying in that narrow iron bed I kept thinking that Django would always be a child, he'd never know what it was to have a woman. Because I had to see humpback whales.

I did the necessary paperwork to get the coffin on the plane and eventually Django and I took off for home. I had an aisle seat next to a young German couple. She was about six months' pregnant, a big sturdy girl like the one in the Schiele painting. He was also large, and both of them had blue eyes and fair hair. He put his hand on her belly and they smiled at each other, then at me. I smiled back and said, '*Viel Gluck.*'

'*Sprechen sie Deutsch?*' said the man.

'No,' I said, 'just the odd word.' I put on my headset and went from one channel to another until I found a male voice with female backing singing:

I'll be waiting on the far side bank of Jordan,
I'll be waiting, drawing pictures in the sand,

And when I see you coming I will rise up with a shout,
And come running through the shallow waters, reaching
   for your hand.

I felt tears rolling down my face and saw the young
couple watching me and looking concerned. I tapped
the headset and said, 'The music.' They nodded and
smiled, feeling sorry for me. Their child would probably be a large boy with fair hair and blue eyes. All
being well, he'd be almost ten now. I imagined him
having a kickabout with his father, could hear the
sound of the ball being kicked and their laughter. All
being well.

   OK, I'm back in the present now. One of the songs
we'll be doing tonight, 'Birdshit on Your Statue', was
written by Jimmy Wicks soon after we came back from
Vienna in 1988:

> Up so high you used to be,
> used to be, used to be –
> Way too high for guys like me,
> Used to be, oh used to be
> Like a statue far above,
> Much too high to ever love
> Guys like me, you used to be.
> But now I see, yes now I see,
> Now I'm noticing that you'
> V'got birdshit on your high statue,
> What a shame, oh what a shame,
> Is it pigeons we should blame?

Birdshit on your statue,
What a shame!

Jimmy's tune for that song and his slide guitar were very snaky, quite vicious. 'Did you have a particular statue in mind?' I asked him.

'Well, you know,' he said, 'if the birdshit fits . . .'

I just let that lie, I didn't really want to get into it with him. He's always wanted to move on me but while he and Tracy were together he couldn't quite work himself up to it, and now that I'm with Elias he's having difficulty handling it. He's been seeing me so much from his point of view that he's never read my total lack of interest in him other than as a colleague. Come to think of it, did I ever read Sid right and did he read me right? The world is full of emotional dyslexics.

Elias Newman, does he want to be a new man for himself and can he be it? And is he the right new man for me? I really wouldn't mind not seeing him for a few days.

14

ELIAS NEWMAN

24 January 2003. The Mobile Mortuary concert didn't start until eight o'clock, so it was already dark when I boarded the 295. This bus turns off Lillie Road into Fulham Palace Road on the way to the Hammersmith Apollo. It used to be the Hammersmith Odeon and is now the *Carling* Hammersmith Apollo. In the phone book it's found under Carling, not Hammersmith. More and more things are under something they didn't use to be under. Beer are the snows of yesteryear.

Once in Fulham Palace Road the 295 unrolled fewer and fewer English shop fronts and more and more multicultural ones. I know that xenophobia dare not speak its name in intellectual circles but I liked it better when the chippies outnumbered the halal. Proceeding grottywise past Charing Cross Hospital and whatever was opposite we arrived by lamplight at the Hammersmith Whatever. Why was I feeling so . . . negative? I'm not a negative sort of person.

Even at night the sky was light enough to show the black loom of the Hammersmith Flyover. It was on the right of an inverted triangle of sky, on the left of which stood the other-century red-brick angularity of College Court, complete with a witch's hat atop its corner.

The forecourt was crowded with an interesting mix of people and a couple of ticket touts whose hyper-activity made them seem ten or more. As this was January, T-shirts were mostly covered by jackets and coats but the bits I saw intrigued me. VE WA was among a group of dangerous-looking men in biker's leathers. T IN M appeared more than once in a patently middle-class cluster. There were young women and some not so young, all in black and sporting white faces, black lipstick, black eye make-up and long lank hair. There were young men in Transylvanian couture and a variety of gothic quiffs. In all of these categories there were some of a grand-parent persuasion and the whole demographic aggreg-ate milled about by lamplight, waiting for the doors to open. There was the usual crowd buzz but nothing very loud.

On the front of the Hammersmith Apollo, topped by quasi-Cecil B. DeMille general-purpose pillars, was a very horizontal marquee that opposed the verticality of College Court and (due to the laws of perspective) the Hammersmith Flyover. MACCABEE ENTER-PRISES & D.O.A. RECORDS PRESENT MOBILE MORTUARY, widely said the front.

'Who the fuck is Maccabee?' said one of the dangerous-looking men to another.

'Jews,' said his colleague.

'Not Scotch?' said Dangerous No. 1.

'Maccabee,' said No. 2, 'as in four-by-twos.'

'Not Scotch?' said No. 1.

'Yids,' said No. 2. 'Non-skids.'

'Fuck,' said No. 1. 'That's the fucking last time *I* vote Labour.'

'I should fucking hope so,' said No. 2. 'Remind me to give you some literature. It'll open your fucking eyes.'

At length the doors opened and we streamed in past the outer minders to the ticket takers in the lobby. There were several bars, a lot of darkness, two mirror-balls reflecting what light they could, and vendors selling T-shirts blazoned with the soles of two bare feet, with a tag that said MOBILE MORTUARY on the left big toe. Also displayed were miniature body drawers containing individual members of the band, decently shrouded up to the shoulders. There were posters in several designs, CDs and videos. Refreshments were available as well.

The miniature Christabel startled me; that I was intimate with a woman who was replicated in this way was unsettling. I looked around me, doing a memory rewind to check that I had come to this by steps that were impulsive but not incomprehensible; all of those steps had been taken because of my belief in a connection that was there before we met and that connection had brought me to the Hammersmith Apollo tonight.

Jackets were more open now and I noted a fair number that said NOT IN MY NAME and WAR IS NOT THE ANSWER. Also present, along with the dangerous men, were a substantial number of enthusiasts whose haircuts suggested that they thought war *was* the answer. The VE WA T-shirt I'd seen before now revealed itself as GIVE WAR A CHANCE. I was made aware, not for the first time, that I was not fully engaged with the world. Certainly I didn't think war with Iraq was a good idea but I'd come here tonight to see and hear Mobile Mortuary and I wasn't expecting David Dimbleby and a discussion on the international situation.

Looking up from where I stood I saw that the lobby was at the bottom of a kind of atrium at the top of which were several tiers of pinkness below the pink ceiling. The stairs on my left offered CIRCLE and LICENSED BAR. Before going up I asked one of the ticket takers if there was a support band.

'Fathoms,' he said.

'Deep?'

'No idea. Next!'

I went up the stairs, gave the licensed bar a miss, and went directly to my seat in the first row of the circle.

I had a good view of the stage where there was no action as yet. The only light was from some art deco ceiling fixtures. The audience murmured, coughed, and shifted in their seats for quite a long time. I had no one to murmur to until the middle-aged man on my left took off his jacket and revealed a T-shirt that said ANAPAESTS FOR PEACE. When he saw me reading it he smiled and said, 'De-de-*dum*?'

'I don't think so,' I said.

'Iambic is the martial metre,' he said: '"The *king* with *half* the *East* at *heel* is *marched* from *lands* of *morning* . . ."'

'"Be*ware* the *Jabberwock*, my *son*! The *jaws* that *bite*, the *claws* that *catch*! . . ."' said the young man on my right, one of the dangerous types I had noticed earlier. He took off his leather jacket and aimed GIVE WAR A CHANCE at the anapaest man who shook his head but said nothing.

After a while there were green and blue-green lights on the stage and a projection of water patterns on a screen. The lighting was dim and I couldn't be sure how many performers constituted Fathoms. They were so close together that they became a single unit from which radiated tentacles of blue light. Their music was very low-frequency and was felt as much as heard, grinding its way up from the bottom of the sea. Their song or chant or whatever was something growled and gutturalised almost below the hearing threshold. The refrain seemed to be, '*Nnvsnu tsrungh, nnvsnu nngh, nnvsnu rrndu ts'irnh ts'irnh ts'irnh nngrh.*'

This was repeated over and over until it filled my mind and I began to feel very deep, very dark, with billions of tons of water bearing down on me. I must have fallen asleep and missed their other numbers, because what I saw next were green, blue, and purple lights playing over clouds of mist rising from the stage. Under a blaze of white light a wall of body drawers appeared, the lighting became a great deal more so, the body drawers slid out and the band emerged from them. There was a blast of many decibels from which Jimmy Wicks separated himself to address the audience. 'Hi!' he said.

'Hi!' said the crowd with whoops and whistles.

'This is a time,' said Jimmy, 'when it's hard to know what it is and what it isn't. So we're going to open with a song for this time: "Did It Wasn't?".' The band went into the intro and Christabel picked up the microphone and sang:

> Did it wasn't, did it was?
> Did we walking in the wasn't,
> did we strolling in the park?
> Did we wasn't in the isn't,
> did we dancing in the dark?
> Did it always, did it never
> have to did it was for ever?
> Did it will or did it won't,
> did it do or did it don't?
> Did it ever come out straight?
> Did it always was too late?
> Am I fuzzy, is there fuzz?
> Did it wasn't, did it was?

When she had only begun the song there were cigarette lighters flaring in the audience and some attempt from the crowd at a backing vocal at varying distances from the beat, rather like the way I used to sing in Music class in elementary school when I followed the lead of the girl in front of me who could read music. I couldn't. I had no trouble with 'A Spanish Cavalier' and 'Juanita' and other schoolroom standards in Morning Exercises but in Music class Miss Schwer was constantly breaking new ground with notes that had to be read. I digress.

The cigarette-lighter bearers were peaceful enough but at this point some of the militant haircuts exposed more GIVE WAR A CHANCE T-shirts; pushing and shoving took place as scuffles broke out. Security people and cooler haircuts quickly prevailed and Christabel finished the song uninterrupted.

The next number was 'Birdshit on Your Statue'. Christabel and the band were only a few bars into this when the middle-aged and bespectacled anapaest devotee next to me rose to his feet and shouted, 'Hear that, *Blair*! 'You be*ware*!' Not surprisingly, this aroused a young haircut to his left whose T-shirt flashed, PEACE IS A 4-LETTER WORD.

'You watch it, you bleeding-heart pacifist!' he said.

'You want *war*?' said the bleeding heart, and kicked him in the shin with a non-prosodic foot. These two now squared off as various T-shirts became active else-where while the music was making the ground shake and the lights rotated their colours over the stage. The anapaestic chap turned out to be something of a milling cove, and in a short time had tapped the haircut's claret. 'Once *more into the breach!*' said the elderly one, lapsing into iambic in his excitement.

'Have you got a handkerchief?' I said to the young orthographer.

'Bloody hell,' he said, and produced one that had seen long service.

'Hold it to your nose and tilt your head back,' I said. 'I don't think we need to call an ambulance.'

'That old bloke is a ringer,' he said. 'He come here looking for a fight.'

'Politics not uncommonly leads to bloodshed,' I said. 'If you can't stand the heat you should get out of the Hammersmith Apollo.'

'You some kind of bleeding heart too?' he said.

'Probably. I'll have to think about it.'

While we were having this dialogue Christabel and the band finished 'Birdshit' to much applause and many cigarette lighters and launched into 'No More World':

When I dialled the speaking clock
I got something of a shock –
it said, 'When you hear the pips
would you kindly read my lips
because the time will be exactly
no more world . . .

This of course provoked further confrontations among the T-shirts but a silence swallowed up the band and the audience as a great weariness overcame me and I sank deep, deep into a blueness that grew darker as I sank. Above me I saw naked Christabel sinking with me deep, deep, deep into the dark. Yes, I thought, it's quiet here, quiet is good.

Then I was back in the Hammersmith Apollo and the noise. I wasn't sure I could stand up but I did, waving both arms while the people behind told me to sit down but I was unable to catch Christabel's eye so I left without further attempts at communication. I made my way past the souvenirs without buying a Mobile Mortuary T-shirt and got out into the air where I just stood breathing in the carbon monoxide for a few moments. What was that all about? I asked myself. What was that with the blueness and the dark? I'm a doctor, for God's sake, I don't take drugs and I don't hallucinate or go into altered states. On the other hand, maybe I'm unable to metabolise the blueness and the dark. But where were they coming from?

I went to the Fulham Palace Road hoping for a taxi but there were none. Shortly a 295 bus appeared and I boarded it. The upper deck was crowded but I was able to rest one buttock next to a fat man who was enjoying a burger and fries out of a styrofoam container. I'll probably see you in my clinic one of these days, I thought. The smell of the grease, the sounds of his eating and the oppression of his bulk soon became too much for me as the lights and colours and names and words on shop fronts blurred past. I got off at Dawes Road and walked the rest of the way home, not bothering to hail the several cabs that passed me. The T-shirts and voices of the audience were still with me and all of the opinions expressed, of whatever persuasion, seemed to me reasonable protests against a world that had gone ugly. War or no war didn't make that much difference – the world was tired and ugly and would grow more tired and more ugly as time went on. And more and more people would turn to greasy burgers and fries, Cokes and candy bars and ice cream and come to my clinic in various stages of hyperglycaemia, obesity and cardiovascular distress.

When I got home I opened the door, took a deep breath of silence, turned on some lights, took my coat off, got *Top Hat* off the video shelf, poured myself some cask-strength Bowmore Islay Malt, added water judiciously, and settled back to watch Fred Astaire and Ginger Rogers. Fred by himself has never interested me much despite the wonderful things he could do; the enchanting Ginger, however, as a partner of independent spirit, gave him importance and validated his masculinity by acknowledging his mastery and following his lead. Seeing the grace and *joie de vivre* of their silvery ghosts as they danced 'Cheek to Cheek' filled me with delight and sadness. When they were alive I was glad to know that somewhere they were among us; when they departed this life they left the world poorer. Their dancing was real. Unlike western stars who perform impossible feats with handguns and western presidents who command hundreds of thousands of expendable stuntmen and women, Fred and

Ginger actually did what they did. With tears running down my face I drank my whisky, finished the film, phoned Christabel at home and at her mobile number, got not-available messages at both numbers, and went to bed.

15

CHRISTABEL ALDERTON

25 January 2003. I was hoping to see Elias in the entertainment suite after the show but he didn't turn up. I was stuck talking to D.O.A. executives, and when I got clear and rang his number I got the answering machine, so he must have already gone to sleep.

I'd especially wanted to talk to him because I'd be flying to Honolulu in the morning. The tenth anniversary of Django's death would be the 30th January and I'd booked my flight a couple of weeks before this. I hadn't told Elias about Django, we hadn't yet got that far. I'd booked a return flight for the 2nd February, so I wasn't going to be gone long, but I wanted to hear Elias's voice before I left.

Every year as the 27th approached I thought of Django as I last saw him and tried to imagine how he'd look now. I'd seen Anthony Hopkins as King Lear at the National some years back, and at the end, when he holds the dead Cordelia in his arms and says:

. . . no, no, no life!
Why should a dog, a horse, a rat, have life,
And thou no breath at all? Thou'lt come no more,
Never, never, never, never, never.

I wept as quietly as I could while everything spun around me and I tried not to faint. I bought a copy of the play and read those lines until they burned themselves into my brain and now I hear them when I'm brushing my teeth, crossing the road, all kinds of moments when I'm not even thinking of my lost boy. Consciously. Now, before my flight to Honolulu, I kept seeing him with the grey sky and the dark sea beyond as he went over the edge.

I put on my Django Reinhardt record and that brought back Django's dead father, Adam Freund. I can't control the pictures in my head, and when the music started I saw Adam shagging the stone sphinx to the tune of 'Limehouse Blues'. 'Nuages' brought back naked Adam, the red lampshade and the spires of the Stephansdom. And 'Herr Oluf'. And Elias. Can a person be a bad-luck carrier and am I one? Up to now, four men (counting Ron) and my son were dead. I've had my share of one-night stands and sport fucking and I don't know if any of those men who didn't mean anything to me ran into the Curse of Christabel. Should I break things off with Elias for his own good? Thinking tired me out and I fell asleep and dreamt that Django was with me. 'Mum,' he said, 'I'm tired. Can we go home now?'

'But we *are* home,' I said, and my voice woke me up. My American Airlines flight was due to leave Heathrow at 11:05 but I was advised to arrive three hours early because of security checks. So I ordered a minicab for 07:15, got to Heathrow Terminal 4 at 07:45, wondered if I should phone Elias, decided it was unlucky, loaded my things on a trolley and joined a very slow-moving check-in queue. I eventually reached the counter, and after assuring the woman that I'd packed my own luggage and nobody had given me anything to take on the plane, asked for an aisle seat towards the rear, got a boarding pass, went through Passport Control and the metal detector, and found myself with about an hour and a half to get through before boarding time.

This is the time of year when I feel like a hermit crab without a shell, exposed and vulnerable. But airports have always been safe houses between what's behind me and what's in front of me. Except of course no place is safe now. In spite of that I like the smell of blankness and carpet shampoo and I like the stale recycled air and the lighting that's neither day nor night. I'm comfortable with my book and my ticket and my boarding pass and all the strangers who are between me and the Erlking, the Cyclops, whatever.

I couldn't help asking myself why, on this tenth anniversary of Django's death, I was going to the place where he died. The answer will sound strange but I guess that's how I am. Strange. My night in the Mini

Hotel in Honolulu International Airport in 1993 had kept me from falling apart and I wanted to be kept from falling apart now. I'd phoned ahead so I knew that the Mini Hotel had been shut down after 9/11 but I thought that just being in the airport overnight might help me get my head straight about Elias. Did I want to drag him into my bad luck or should I turn him loose?

I had an Aroma coffee and went to WH Smith to get a book. I was thinking of Donna Leon's latest but *The Woman in Black* by Susan Hill saw me first and jumped into my hand. I don't have to buy this, I thought, I'll just glance at the first couple of pages to see what it's like. But after the opening lines of the first chapter, 'Christmas Eve', it refused to let go of me and I was afraid I'd finish the whole thing before we took off, so I'd need another book for the ten hours to Los Angeles and somehow I missed Donna Leon and was waylaid by Alice Munro's *Hateship, Friendship, Courtship, Loveship, Marriage*. Covering all that, it had to be value for money, so I bought it.

I found a seat with a good view of the monitor screens and noticed that there was a Middle-Eastern-looking man three seats away in the same row. Three seats on the other side of him were also vacant. He was reading an Arabic paper and I wondered if there was any way of spotting a suicide bomber just by looking at him. I probably look suicidal as often as not; lots of people with thoughtful faces might be about to do anything at all.

Boarding was at 10:40, and at 10:15 I rang Elias on my mobile. 'Hello?' he said.

'Hi. It's me. I was hoping to see you last night.'

'I was hoping to see you too, but the debate on the international situation was too much for me so I left. I tried to reach you on your mobile but you weren't available.'

'I'm sorry, but I was surrounded by record company execs and by the time I got away you weren't available either.'

'So anyhow, can we meet tomorrow?'

'That's why I wanted to see you after the gig. I'm at Heathrow now. My flight's leaving soon and I'll be gone for a few days, back on the 2nd February.'

'What are you doing at Heathrow? Where are you going?'

'Honolulu and Maui. It's nothing that's happening now, it's to do with the past — a kind of remembrance day. I'll tell you about it when I get back.' I couldn't quite say what I wanted to say next.

'What?' he said after a few seconds.

'How do you feel about luck?' I said.

'Some days I feel lucky, some I don't. How about you?'

'Sometimes I feel unlucky. Sometimes I feel like a bad-luck carrier.'

'You're not. Finding you has been the luckiest thing that's happened to me in a long time.' Pause. 'I miss you when you're not here. When does your return flight get in? I'll meet you at Heathrow.'

'Don't do that – with two long flights and a stopover at LA there are bound to be delays. I'll come straight to you when I arrive, leave a key for me in case you're out.'

'Yes! I'll leave a key under the right-hand box tree, under the pot so you can let yourself in any time of the day or night.'

'Right. I'll see you soon then.'

'Yes. Please fly carefully.'

'I'll try. See you soon, God willing.' I did a phone kiss and rang off. I'd never said 'God willing' before. I hadn't given him a phone kiss before either. Now I almost didn't want to go.

16

ELIAS NEWMAN

25 January 2003. 'A kind of remembrance day,' she said. Whom was Christabel remembering? Sid Horstmann? A wave of unreasoning jealousy swept over me but then it subsided and left me with the blueness and the dark that had come to me last night at the Hammersmith Apollo. This Saturday was a working day for me: I had a neuropathy piece to finish for the *Lancet* as well as my aetiology notes to organise. I'm a very disciplined person but today the discipline wasn't working – I put on a coat and a woollen hat and muffler and went out into the cold and the greyness.

I walked up the New King's Road and the King's Road to Beaufort Street, then down to the Embankment. The wind was making wavelets on the river and the sailboats and power boats were rocking at their moorings. I headed towards the Albert Bridge, and as I approached the bronze Daphne I was passed by a jogger who reached her before I did, slapped her on the bottom, and rapidly grew small in the distance. 'Cheek,' I said aloud.

There's a bench near the statue, and I sat down and looked at the bridge. Over troubled water, I thought. Sixty-two was hardly an age to think of new beginnings but Christabel might at this very moment be flying away from me to keep a date with the dead and I didn't want her to be away from me.

27 January 2003. BIO-WAR SUITS FOUND IN LONDON MOSQUE, thundered *The Sunday Times*. Next to that was a smaller headline: 'Bush to secure Baghdad after Saddam ousted.' Good luck to us all, I thought. I put the paper down, wondering where Christabel was this morning. She left yesterday morning around 11:00. Figure two ten-hour flights plus a three-hour stopover in Los Angeles – that would put her in Honolulu today, maybe even on her way to Maui by now.

Here it was another cold grey day. After breakfast and a second cup of tea I put on Sonny Terry and Brownie McGhee and listened to their version of 'Midnight Special'. That didn't do it for me so I went to 'Sonny's Squall' and that didn't do it either. I tried 'Just a Closer Walk with Thee' and that was better although it wasn't Jesus I wanted to walk with. I ended up with 'Freight Train' and that one did it for me. Here I was, a respected consultant, and I felt that my life was a train that I had no ticket to ride. I was riding the blinds or, worse than that, riding the rods and

97

holding on for dear life while the sleepers and rails and the roadbed rushed backwards beneath me. 'It's a long low rail and a short cross tie,' I sang along with them. 'Ride the rods till the day I die, just don't tell 'em what train I'm on and they won't know what route I've gone.'

Then I turned off the CD player and dug up the notebook I'd used when I was writing poetry. Had it come to that? It seems it had. I wrote:

> Under the ocean deep and deep,
> remembering nothing, dead owls weep.

'Please, Rodney,' I said, 'you're embarrassing me.' I shook my head to clear it, dressed up warmly and went out for another walk. After a while I found myself on Putney Bridge. Below me the tide was out, the river had narrowed and the mud had widened. The wind was riffling the water, the sky was grey, the wind was cold. A rower in a single shell appeared from under the bridge and his oars walked him across the water and away. I thought of drowned cities, went home, opened a bottle of French Full Red, and watched *Deliverance* on video. I made a cheese omelette, finished the bottle, and settled down to do a little work on the neuropathy piece. Very little.

27 January 2003. Monday morning I put on my professional identity as Elias Newman, Diabetes Consultant, and did my regular round with Registrar Titus Smart,

Senior House Officer Istvakar Rana, House Officer
Brendan Yee, Clinical Pharmacist Winston Davies, and
medical students Nancy Kwan and Elizabeth Yonghe,
a vigorous team of fully shod verticals looking in on
the barefoot horizontals in our care in various wards.

In Bay B of Samuel Plimsoll, in Bed 3 by the
window, was Abraham Selby, a burly black man with
a rugged face and an ironic smile. The grey daylight
illuminating him was, like hospital food, not quite the
same as what you get outside. He was reclining against
several pillows with his left leg elevated by a stack of
folded blankets and a couple of towels. As we
approached he put down *The Times*. 'Ah,' he said, 'Job's
comforters.'

Brendan Yee read from his notes: 'Mr Selby is fifty-
six, insulin dependent with a long-standing history of
Type 1 diabetes. There is diabetic polyneuropathy. He
suffers from ischaemic heart disease, had a coronary
thrombosis in 1993 and a triple bypass in 1994. He was
admitted on the twenty-first of January with cellulitis
in his left leg. He is being treated with intravenous
benzylpenicillin and flucloxacillin, also prophylactic
heparin to reduce the risk of DVTs.'

'How are you feeling?' I asked Selby.

'Overloaded,' he said.

'I know the IV is a bother and clearing this up is a
slow business but the antibiotics will do the job.'

He nodded in a resigned way. 'Oh yes,' he said. 'Do
you believe in God?'

'Why do you ask?'

He showed me a photograph in *The Times*, a close-up of a bat with long ears and a thoughtful face. I'd noticed the picture in my own *Times* when I was having breakfast and I'd been thinking about it. Selby said, 'I'm wondering if His eye is on the bat.'

'I'll have to get back to you on that,' I said.

'Sure you will. I'll be here.'

After the round I surprised him by appearing at his bedside again. He handed me the paper and I reread the caption under the bat portrait which identified the animal as a European free-tailed bat. It had come down, 'exhausted, starving, and injured', in a Cornwall grave-yard. 'It is believed it had been blown off course from its migration route to the Iberian peninsula', wrote the reporter, Simon de Bruxelles. He went on to say that 'European free-tailed bats are high fliers and have been spotted by airline pilots several miles up'.

'"Nineteen-inch wingspan,"' I read. 'That's a pretty big bat.'

'That's what you could call a batline,' said Selby. 'Bat Air, last of the independents. Pilot sitting in his 747 looks out of his window and there's Bat Air flapping along beside him. What's Bat Air doing up there with the big guys?'

'Migrating, it says here.'

'But why so high?'

'I don't know. Maybe it's picking up a favourable air stream.'

'I think there's more to it than that. What if those are souls flying up there?'

'Why would souls take the form of bats?'

'Maybe when you die you stop being separate from every other animal. Maybe you take on a bat shape or a wolf shape or an elephant shape or a whale shape. Maybe the world is full of souls walking or swimming or flying around, and when some of those animals get extinct, those souls die. What if that, eh? Think about it.'

I did.

17

ABRAHAM SELBY

25 January 2003. What I like about Dr Newman is that he makes me feel a little less horizontal. He might be working too hard though, and not getting enough sleep. On his way out of the ward he walked into a bucket one of the cleaners was using and he almost fell over.

18

ANNELIESE NEWMAN

25 January 2003. Sometimes now I dream of music.
Not opera music, what it is I don't know. Over me,
under me, all around me. I can hear it, I can feel it.
When I wake up it is gone. Lost, nothing remembered.

19

CHRISTABEL ALDERTON

25 January 2003. 'The Girl from Ipanema' treacled down the aisles as if a big can of bossa nova in the galley had sprung a leak. I know that the international airport in Rio was named after Antonio Carlos Jobim after his death but I don't think he acquired post-humous performance rights in public conveyances worldwide. The 777 was no more than half full but people still managed to get in each other's way as they found their seats and put things in the overhead compartments.

I was in 28C and I wasn't surprised to find that the swarthy man between the empty seats in the depar-ture lounge was next to me. We were on the left-hand side, about halfway back in Economy. I was aisle, he was middle, and window was a very fat man who smelled like Burger King and breathed heavily. Because Mr Window overflowed his space Mr Middle's right arm sometimes pressed against my left arm. He smiled apologetically and made himself small. Then he took out a string of worry beads and began to worry them.

The flight attendants did their thing with pointing out the emergency exits and demonstrating the life jackets, we hung about for a while queueing for take-off, then the 777 got serious, pulled itself together, started rolling, gathered speed and let go of the ground. London tilted away below us and the drinks trolley slowly, slowly arrived. I had two gin and tonics, the worrying man had orange juice and the fat man had two Diet Pepsis. The captain told us about the weather and how high we'd be flying and how long it would take, then we all settled back to breathe the low-oxygen air and wait for lunch. I like those little time-outs between what you've just left behind and what's waiting up ahead; they never last long enough.

I opened *The Woman in Black*. This was a really classy ghost story of the old-fashioned kind. The Alice Munro book had a bright cover and seemed to have at least one story with a happy ending but the ghost story pulled me first. I was just settling into the atmosphere of it when lunch came and I had *coq au vin* and some white wine. After lunch I had a bit of a kip and then got well stuck in to Eel Marsh and Nine Lives Causeway and the tides and weathers of the story which took me up to the next drinks, followed by Dover sole and more white wine.

By then the overhead lights were switched off and it was movie time. The menu for the screen on the back of the seat in front gave me several choices including a remake of *Solaris*. I've never seen a good remake and I wasn't going to watch this one but the title brought back something of the original film that I saw years ago. I remembered water and the sound of water, water in a stream, running over reeds, water in a pond, frozen in winter, water coming down in rain. And then there was the ocean on the planet Solaris. This ocean didn't actually have water in it but a kind of plasma that reacted to what was in the minds of the men in the space station above it. It took their thoughts and memories and it made copies of people in their lives and sent them up to the station. These were flesh and blood just like the originals. The psychologist at the station was visited by what seemed to be his wife who'd killed herself ten years before. She was confused and frightened – she didn't know what she was. She couldn't bear to let him out of her sight, even broke through a steel door to be with him. At first he was so spooked by this that he put her in a rocket and shot her off, but the next day she was back. She loved him and he loved her too, even though he knew she wasn't really real. 'Love can only be experienced, it can't be explained,' he said. When the replica finally understood what she was she tried to commit suicide but failed. Poor thing – how real is anybody, really? I tried to recall the ending but I couldn't. I know it was sad.

We were over the ocean while I was remembering *Solaris*. O God! I thought, if only the ocean beneath us could send up my dead son, alive and well, even if it was only a copy of him, but a warm and breathing

Django I could hold in my arms and he would call me Mum.

The swarthy man touched my arm. 'You all right?' he said.

'Yes,' I said. 'Why?'

'You crying,' he said.

I put a hand to my face. My cheeks were wet. 'Eye-strain,' I said. 'Too much reading.'

'Me too,' he said.

'Reading too much?'

He shook his head. 'Too much sad.'

'How come?'

'Dead. Gone for ever.'

'Who?'

He shook his head again and put his hand over his heart. 'Name is like gravestone in little cemetery inside me,' he said. 'I take flowers, go alone.'

'Me too,' I said. 'Little cemetery inside me.'

'Yes,' he said. 'Too much sad.' He went back to his beads.

The last time I flew into LAX was for a gig at the House of Blues in Hollywood. We had electrical problems with the light rig and the show wasn't one of our best. As the plane tilted I saw Los Angeles all spread out and sprawling and it just had a flat noplace look. Places do that for me, they change sometimes from one hour to the next; maybe another time it would've looked like someplace.

After my arrival at Terminal 4 of the Tom Bradley International Terminal there was a three-hour stopover before I changed planes for the flight to Honolulu. As always in airports there were bodied voices and disembodied ones. The bodied ones accompanied the swarming footsteps and the disembodied ones tried to find people. Señor Manuel Losano was being paged in English and Spanish. No one's looking for me, I thought. What if I just stayed here and didn't make any more decisions. But of course doing that would require a decision.

I had a club sandwich and several coffees sitting outside a Daily Grill restaurant that had SATISFAC-TION SERVED DAILY over its front. I thought that was a pretty big claim and I noticed that satisfaction wasn't on the menu. I wandered around a little, bought a pair of Gucci sunglasses at the Sunglass Hut, and did a quick browse at WH Smith, which I was surprised to see so far from home. In the window there was a big display of *Dianetics* by L. Ron Hubbard. L. Ron Hubbard! I'd thought he'd had his day and was long gone but here his book was, alive and well in LA. The Scientologists used to have a shop-front recruiting operation in Tottenham Court Road where they tried to get people inside for some kind of testing that involved tin cans as I remember. I guess the California climate favours Scientology and of course they've got Tom Cruise and John Travolta which can't hurt sales. Nobody pulled me in for a tin-can test so I got away from there and walked about smelling stale fries and watching people coming from wherever they'd been and going to wherever they'd be next.

There were monitors everywhere with flights that weren't mine and announcements on the tannoy that had nothing to do with me.

I went halfway down the stairs to the Mezzanine to look at something I'd passed on my way up. At first glance it was like the large diagrams you see in the London Underground but it had moving parts. It was like a pinball machine stood on its side, up on easel legs like a lecturer's blackboard, and you couldn't do anything with it but watch it doing its own thing with balls dropping from one level to another in different ways and bells ringing as if it was demonstrating a pattern of meaningless events for no particular reason. 'You talking to me?' I said.

A woman with a small boy came along. Tight jeans, pink trainers, pink T-shirt that said LONG TIME GONE, big frizzy hair, unlit fag in her mouth, sunglasses. The boy was wearing a camouflage outfit. He might have been ten or eleven but looked old beyond his years. 'Wait,' he said, 'it's some kind of game.'

'OK,' said the woman, 'so where's the joysticks?'

'Maybe it's the kind you hold in your hand, only bigger,' said the boy. They both studied it for a while and said, 'Tsss.' The woman had taken off her sunglasses and I saw that she had a black eye.

She put the glasses back on and turned to me. 'Have you figured this thing out?'

'Not yet,' I said.

'No buttons to push,' she said. She and the boy tried pressing the glass in various places with no result.

'Stupid thing,' said the boy. 'You can't do anything with it.'

'That's life,' said the woman, and they moved on.

I found myself humming one of the old Nectarine numbers I'd written, 'A Long Way Down'.

I was high on the love we'd found,
and now it's such a long way down . . .

It was raining the day Dick Turpin lost his footing on a roof and it was raining the day of his funeral. Dick's mother was there, also his brother and Mrs Brother. Brother gave me a hard look and Mrs looked away. She was wearing a skirt as short as mine but she didn't have the legs for it. Dick hadn't ever made a will, so I got everything. I'd certainly earned it, and with his bank account plus the sale of the house and the business, I'd be able to set myself up comfortably in London and sleep in a bed that would never have anybody in it that I didn't want.

'I am the resurrection and the life, saith the Lord,' said the vicar; 'he that believeth in me, though he were dead, yet shall he live . . .' I didn't recall that Dick had any belief in Jesus and I doubted that Jesus believed in Dick. When the vicar got to 'We brought nothing into this world and it is certain we can carry nothing out' I nodded my head yes and wondered what I'd ever have that I wouldn't want to leave behind. Now I was humming 'Nuages' and I shook my head and went back to my book.

The Woman in Black is only 160 pages but it was slow reading because I kept stopping and thinking my thoughts before going back to the page I was on. Some of it I read again and again, like the part where the narrator hears the sound of a ghostly pony trap, then the neighing of the horse and the cry of a child as they get sucked into the marsh.

I got to the end eventually and it left me with a feeling of dread. So why had I carried on to the end? Good question.

The plane for Honolulu was a 757 but the drinks trolley was the same size as the one on the 777. I didn't bother with the movies or the headphone music and I didn't start the Alice Munro book. I closed my eyes and listened to the whale music in my head and watched Django go over the edge of the cliff. This time it was a woman next to me who said, 'Are you all right?' American.

'Why?' I said.

'You're crying.'

'No,' I said, 'it's just that my eyes water a lot when I've had a few drinks.'

'Oh,' she said, nodding to show that she understood. She was young and pretty, with long dark hair and a serious face and just a little bit of that bulldog jaw some pretty young Americans have. 'I don't feel too happy myself. I was down in San Diego visiting my boyfriend. He'll be shipping out for the Gulf soon.'

'Army?'

'Navy. He's training dolphins to clear mines.' She

took out her wallet and showed me a photograph of a smiling man in a boat and a smiling dolphin leaping out of the water beside it.

'Nice-looking guy,' I said. 'The dolphin looks happy. I'd have thought they were too smart to muck about with mines.'

'Leroy – that's my boyfriend's name – he says they're smart but they think it's cool to hang out with humans. So they'll do all kinds of things for a few fish, just to be buddies with their trainers.'

'Does he just send them down to do the work or does he go down with them?'

'He says he won't have to get into the water with them once they've learnt what to do but I don't believe him. I think about him over there, down in dark and muddy water with his dolphin. Either of them makes a mistake and Whammo! that's all she wrote.'

'Isn't there still a chance that war won't happen?'

'It'll happen. Bush thinks with his dick. He's got all those planes and ships and tanks and bombs and he's got a hard-on for Saddam Hussein. If it wasn't Saddam it'd be somebody else. A while back it was Osama Bin Laden but you don't hear much about him any more.' She stopped talking but her lips were moving while we flew over banks of white clouds that looked as if you could walk on them if you were careful. Far down below was the sea.

'I had a dream about Leroy,' she said. 'I must have been underwater. The water was very clear and I could see him swimming toward me. But there were trees between us, thin trees not all that close together but he couldn't get through.'

'What happened then?'

'I woke up with my heart beating fast. What do you think it meant?'

'Well, there's the thing with Iraq standing between you. And you could say you won't be out of the woods until it's cleared up.'

Her right hand was rubbing the third finger of her left hand, like a close-up in a movie. 'I want us to get married before he ships out,' she said, 'but Leroy isn't sure. He's very superstitious and he says it's like asking for something to happen and I'll be the widow who gets the folded-up flag at the funeral. But if we don't get married and it happens, then I'll always think, at least we could have had that, at least I'd be his widow instead of just a grieving girlfriend.'

'I'm superstitious too,' I said. 'I think if you get married it might keep him safe.'

Her face lit up. 'I'll tell him that,' she said. 'Thank you. My name's Elizabeth.'

'I'm Christabel.' We shook hands. The captain announced that we were about to begin our descent. The sound of the engines changed and my ears popped. The sky was grey and so was the ocean.

Honolulu tilted into view with white buildings and soon the wheels touched the ground and we kept our seat belts fastened and the backs of our seats upright and so on until finally the captain thanked us for flying American and the time was now ten hours earlier than it was in London. 'Are you here for business or pleasure?' Elizabeth said to me as we left the plane.

'Visiting a friend,' I said. 'You?'

'Delivering ashes,' she said, 'to my grandparents. My mom and dad died on 9/11. They were born here and this is the first chance I've had to bring them home.'

'Sorry,' I said.

She nodded a couple of times. 'Thanks,' she said. 'You have to move on.'

20

ELIZABETH BARTON

25 January 2003. That woman who sat next to me on the plane, Christabel, she was crying all right. I had a feeling about her, like that shudder you get when somebody walks over your grave. What she said about keeping Leroy safe by getting married, I wasn't so sure about that. I didn't think she knew anything about keeping anybody safe. When we were over the water I did 'Eternal Father, Strong To Save' like I always do, singing it in my head:

> Eternal Father, strong to save,
> Whose arm hath bound the restless wave,
> Who biddest the mighty ocean deep
> Its own appointed limits keep;
> Oh, hear us when we cry to Thee,
> For those in peril on the sea!

I just do the first verse. I don't think God needs the whole thing every time.

21

ELIAS NEWMAN

28 January 2003. I dreamt about a dog we had when I was a boy. Bo, we called him, short for Boris. He was a cross between a German shepherd and a collie, and my father used to walk him twice a day. He was about as old as I was, very quiet and well-mannered except that when he was off the leash he chased cars. One finally hit him the year after my father died. My sisters nursed him devotedly; they didn't want to lose my father's dog but his injuries were too severe and he had to be put down. I hadn't thought about him for the last fifty years or so but here he was in a dream. He was very old and stiff but he took the leash in his mouth and went to the door and looked back at me. 'Bo!' I said, 'Poor old Bo!' and woke up to a grey day with a cold wind blowing.

For a moment I didn't know where I was but I felt that something was missing. Then it came back to me – Christabel was on her way to Hawaii for her remembrance day. Yet another mystery. There were always new unknowns with her. In an effort to get my mind off her I phoned Peter Diggs and arranged to meet him for lunch.

I did a morning clinic, then I went to meet Peter at The Daniel Mendoza off Long Acre. I'd first heard about it from a patient who was a betting man with a keen interest in all sporting events. He strongly regretted that boxing had become what he called a namby-pamby sport and claimed that he had several times seen the real (and illicit) bare-knuckle thing. Being Jewish he longed for a new Daniel Mendoza to rise like the golem and show the gentiles how it was done. The restaurant is a dark brown place with prints of Mendoza and other bare-knuckle boxers: Tom Cribb, Jem Belcher, Deaf Burke, Ben Caunt, Bendigo and so on. Also Pierce Egan and various of the Fancy. 'Patronised by HRH the Prince of Wales 1792,' said the wooden banner over the bar. A framed poster showed Mendoza coming up to scratch under the words, in large capitals, MENDOZA THE JEW, HEAVYWEIGHT CHAMPION OF ENGLAND. There were several pen-and-ink portraits in which he looked more a poet than a bruiser. Although only five foot seven and a middleweight, he defeated much bigger men to become heavyweight champion and is credited with being the father of scientific boxing. He wore his hair long and curly, possibly with Samson in mind, but this proved his downfall in a bout with 'Gentleman' John Jackson who grabbed him by his hair and gave him a beating from which his status never recovered.

There was a clatter of cutlery and glassware and a clamour of high-cholesterol smells and conversation, much of the latter in Yiddish, with gestures. My people.

'You come here often?' said Peter.

'From time to time when I need cheering up,' I said, and I told him about the dream. 'It was so vivid! I could even smell his old-dog smell, Bo looking up at me with a dried-up trickle from each eye – I keep wondering what it means.'

'Well,' said Peter, 'are you an old dog wanting someone to take you walkies?'

'All the time, but there was more to it than that.'

Peter looked at the ceiling, low and dark brown, with beams. 'Of course, this may very well be Bo's dream that you found yourself in.'

'Bo is a dead dog,' I said.

'So? Who can say where dreams begin and end, and where they travel from and to?'

'You're strange,' I said.

'Everybody's strange, only most people try to cover it up.'

A heavyweight waiter wearing a yarmulke arrived and we both ordered potato pancakes. 'Latkes twice,' he said, and wrote it down. 'Anything to drink with that?'

'What kind of beer have you got?' said Peter.

'Maccabee,' said the waiter.

'Haven't heard of that one,' said Peter.

'You're not Jewish, right?'

'Right.'

'The Maccabees killed a lot of goyim. So we have Maccabee beer.'

'Bottled or draft?'

'Bottled.'

'But I can see beer pumps at the bar.'

'Those are from a long time ago, never been taken out. Should I sit down and we'll have a conversation or would you like to give me your beer decision?'

'OK,' said Peter, 'I'll have a Maccabee.'

'Make it two,' I said.

The waiter wrote down our order, frowned, shook his head, and withdrew.

'I haven't had this one before,' I said.

'Bare-knuckle waiting, would you call it?' said Peter.

'He's a Jewish waiter,' I said. 'It's a role that's heavy with tradition and he's doing it the traditional way. Where were we?'

'Being strange.'

'Right. You said that Bo was quiet and well-mannered but he chased cars, was hit by one and had to be put down. Did he have a death wish or what? Now he's pulled you into his dream in which he's old and you're sixty-two and he wants to take you for a walk. Do you want to go with him?'

'Peter, Bo's dead, OK?'

'Well, of course he's dead – that's not the sort of dream a live dog would have. *Are* you going to walk with him?'

'If he dreams me again I'll let you know what

happens. What are you doing since your big success with "Death and the Maiden"?'

'I'm still involved with that theme and doing more sketches and paintings. It's a toughie, it's so full of ambiguities. The thing about "Death and the Maiden" is that they need each other. Redon did a wonderful lithograph in his *Temptation of Saint Anthony* series in which they're both full-frontal naked, although Death is more naked because he's in his bones. The Maiden is rising above him like a fire balloon but he's got hold of her arm with one bony hand and she won't get away. The incandescence of her body lights up the air around her but her face is shadowed by night and Death has a firm grip. He's very pleased with himself; in the caption he says to her, 'It is I who make you serious. Let us embrace each other.' He's so full of himself that he doesn't realise that she makes *him* serious too. Without her youth and beauty on which to exercise his *droit du mort* he's nothing but a Hallowe'en costume. Niklaus Manuel Deutsch, 400 years before Redon, draws the maiden fully clothed but showing a lot of cleavage and not putting up much resistance while Death slides his tongue into her mouth and his hand up her skirt. The permutations are endless.'

'Maccabees,' said our waiter, plunking two bottles on the table.

'No glasses?' said Peter.

The waiter pointed to the slices of lemon stuck in the mouths of the bottles. 'That's how we do it,' he said, and left.

'You drink it through the lemon,' I said.

'Seems very effete for a bare-knuckle place,' said Peter.

'This is a very cosmopolitan establishment,' I said. 'How many paintings have you done so far in the new series?'

'Three, but nothing finished – I've been papering the walls with sketches as I gradually get my chops together.'

'I thought "chops" was a musician word.'

'I got it from Amaryllis but the word isn't limited to music – it means skills, technique, or talents of any kind.'

'Sometimes my chops are a little bit scattered,' I said. 'This morning at the clinic I found it hard to stay interested. How's Amaryllis?'

'Fine. She's into composing now, working on a Cthulhu suite. *The Dream of R'lyeh* is the first part.'

'How does it sound?'

'Oceanic. The mode is Lydian in a non-Euclidean sort of way if you know what I mean.'

'Not yet, but I can wait till it comes to me.'

A man at the next table paused with a forkful of gefilte fish halfway to his mouth and turned to Peter. 'What,' he said, 'You're supporting Gaddafi now?'

'I said Lydian, not Libyan,' said Peter.

'I don't know from Lydians,' said the gefilte man, 'but if they want to start something Israel is ready for them.'

'Thank you for your input,' said Peter. 'I feel easier in my mind now.'

'There is no mental ease these days,' said the man, and went back to his fish.

'Amaryllis is known for her volatility,' I said to Peter. 'How is she to live with?'

'I'm pretty volatile myself, so we get along all right. In any case, the whole thing between men and women is a very dodgy business. Have you seen Christabel Alderton since the Royal Academy?'

'Yes.'

'I thought you might. Are you going to say more?'

'Not yet.'

'OK, be prudent.'

'Latkes twice,' said our waiter, plunking down two plates which sent up strong feel-good aromas. Also a dish of sour cream. 'Enjoy,' he said.

'Thank you,' said Peter. 'I'm sure we shall. By the way?'

'Yes?' said the waiter.

'I saw the bartender working a beer pump,' said Peter.

'Oh, that,' said the waiter.

'Yes?' said Peter.

'That's Masada bitter. I wasn't sure you'd like it.'

'Could I have a pint? I don't want to be pushy.'

'My pleasure, sir,' said the waiter.

'Make it two,' I said.

'You got it,' said the waiter. 'My name is Moe.'

'Nice to meet you, Moe,' said Peter. 'This is Elias and I'm Peter.' We shook hands.

'You I've seen before,' said Moe, nodding to me.

'You do any boxing?' said Peter.

'When I was younger. This is what I do now, plus I get extra work in movies from time to time. I'll bring your Masadas.'

When the bitter appeared Peter sampled it and said, 'It's bitter all right.'

'That's why it's called Masada,' said Moe. 'It's an acquired taste. Have you read Josephus, *The Jewish Wars*?'

'No,' said Peter.

'Do,' said Moe. 'You'll like our bitter better next time.'

The cosiness of The Daniel Mendoza made the day seem colder and greyer when we were outside again. At Covent Garden Peter went to browse the Jubilee Market. I whistled to Bo and we disappeared into the Piccadilly Line.

22

CHRISTABEL ALDERTON

25 January 2003. I was glad to see the last of Elizabeth and her ashes. I was beginning to think I had LET'S TALK ABOUT DEATH tattooed on my forehead. Or maybe it was just written on my face. Ashes. Two black horses drew Django's black-plumed hearse to the Golders Green Crematorium. 'Nuages' was the music as the beautiful coffin that Rudy Ka'uhane had made went through the doors. Later I was given a little urn of ashes. I scattered them over the Thames near the Albert Bridge just as the tide was going out.

After going through customs I came out into the main lobby with the other arrivals. My footsteps joined the other footsteps and I listened as they took me back to 1993.

Although I knew that the Mini Hotel Sleep/Shower had been shut down I went to have a look anyhow. There it was, chained and padlocked, still with signs by the entrance showing the room rates. A hand-lettered sign on the door: AS OF TODAY (10/15/01) WE

ARE NOT LONGER OPEN FOR BUSINESS. MAHALO!!! Looking through the glass I could see various rubbish and debris, fallen ceiling tiles, some partitions, a stool, an old map on the floor. It had been such a quiet place, and now it seemed noisy with emptiness. I imagined my ghost beating its fists against the glass while I stood there listening to footsteps and echoes and smelling fries from where the Fresh Express cafeteria used to be. Now there's a food court with Burger King, Pizza Hut Express, Chinese fast food and a bakery with coffee and ice cream. If aliens from outer space ever want to visit us they could home in on the smells from Burger King and Pizza Hut. Maybe they already have, and now they staff those establishments and say 'Have a good day' like regular people.

In London it would be almost nine o'clock in the morning; here it was getting on for ten in the evening of the night before London's morning. So I was really in yesterday but that's nothing new. I had coffee and pineapple ice cream while the people around me from yesterday or tomorrow had whatever it was time for by their reckoning.

Through the glass I could see the spotlit gardens and the little Chinese pagoda. I visited the ladies' and remembered the air freshener of 1993 with its Juicy Fruit fragrance. Now there was just a blank smell. Then I went out to the Japanese garden and sat under the gazebo there. It was raining a little by then, and the drops pattered on the roof and on the leaves and splashed in the ponds. It was a good sound and the rain was like a time freshener with a smell of tomorrows.

I must have been sitting there for quite a while when I heard another sound. Then I saw something on the ground that flapped a little and stopped. I went to it and saw that it was a bat, strange and furry, the fur not like a mouse but like a proper little flying animal. It seemed dead but I was afraid to touch it.

I was standing there looking at it when a very large security man with a gun appeared. 'Everything all right?' he said.

I pointed to the bat. 'It just dropped out of the air,' I said. 'Is it dead?'

He knelt to examine it. '*Ope'ape'a*,' he said. 'It's dead all right. They're not as rare as they were a while back but they're still an endangered species.'

'What did you call it?'

'*Ope'ape'a* is the Hawaiian name. Hoary bat is what it's called in English. *Lasiurus cinereus semotus* is the scientific name. It's Hawaii's only bat.'

'How do you know so much about it?'

'I'm a member of the Sierra Club and we have a project to save this bat. Look how beautiful it is.' He held it up by its outspread wings. Its fur was grey, with a cream-coloured ruff around the head. Long ears and sharp teeth.

'What killed it?' I said. 'Why did it fall out of the air right here in front of me? Do you think it was sick?'

'No idea. I'll take it to the university, there's a man

there who can do an autopsy.' He took off his cap and put the bat in it. 'Bat in a hat,' he said.

'Is it a male?'

'Yes. How come you asked?'

'No reason. Do you think it's unlucky if a bat drops dead in front of you?'

'Look at it this way: this bat got to the end of his run and he picked you for his crash landing. Most people never get to see an *Ope'ape'a*, so this makes you special.'

'Like a beacon for dying bats?'

'Try to think positive – maybe he was picking up good vibrations from you. Maybe he knew you'd keep him in your thoughts and remember him. Have you got a camera with you?'

'Yes.'

'So you should take some pictures.'

'To capture this dead-bat moment?'

'It's a moment you'll want to look at again.'

'OK.' I took one of him holding the bat and another closer one of the bat in his hands.

'Here,' he said, 'I'll take one of you with the bat.' I gave him the camera and held up the bat and he did it. And came in for a second one, a close-up of my face. He was a nice-looking Hawaiian with a lot of charm.

'I don't need to remember what I look like,' I said.

'I do,' he said. 'My name is Henry Panawae.'

'Henry, are you hitting on me? I'm old enough to be your mother.'

'A woman like you is special,' he said. 'Age don't matter. 'Your name?'

'Christabel Alderton.' He was around thirty-five or so. The kind of man a woman says yes to. 'You're probably married with a couple of kids,' I said.

'For sure,' he said, 'but if I wasn't.'

'You've made me feel twenty years younger. Thank you.'

'My pleasure,' he said.

'If you give me your address I'll send you prints.'

He wrote down his name and his address on a note-book page that he tore off and gave me and I wrote down mine for him. It was raining harder so we got under the gazebo. 'I make a circle around this day on my calendar,' he said.

'Me too.' And I did. The circle is there now. And he and the bat are in my photo album. A moment I look at sometimes.

'You going to be here a while?' he said.

'Yes. I'll get a morning flight to Maui but I'll be around all night. Later I'll go to the lounge.'

'OK, I'll see you later then. I'll be going on my rounds now.' He turned to go, then stopped. 'We never said hello properly,' he said.

'OK. Hello, Henry.'

'Better we do it the old way, which is called *honi*: we touch foreheads, we look into each other's eyes which is where the soul looks out, then with nose to nose we mingle our breath.'

I knew about *honi* because I'd done it in 1993 with

Rudy Ka'uhane and his wife but I felt like teasing Henry. 'That's going pretty far with a stranger,' I said.

'Nobody's a stranger, that's what it's all about, OK?'

So we touched foreheads and his thoughts were next to mine; we looked into each other's eyes and I could see he was a man you could depend on; we mingled our breath and he wasn't a stranger.

He left and I sat there for another hour or so, smelling the rain and listening to it on the roof and the leaves and the water of the ponds. I wondered what Elias was doing and whether he was thinking of me. I'd never looked straight into his eyes as closely as I did with Henry's.

23

HENRY PANAWAE

28 January 2003. That woman, Christabel Alderton, she was sad. Lot of trouble in her eyes. But she was special, maybe she'll be all right. I hope so. *Ope'ape'a* picked her.

24

ELIAS NEWMAN

28 January 2003. When I left Peter and went down to the netherworld of the Piccadilly Line with the ghost of Bo padding after me I found myself remembering Mary Snyder, a girl I had a crush on when I was fourteen. I'm not sure how Bo led me to her but there she was. She was very pretty, with blue eyes, fair hair and a face that I've seen on porcelain figures. I got her to go fishing with me one summer day. I cycled over to her place in Kulpsville or maybe it was Souderton and we rode to a nice little tree-shaded part of the Perkiomen Creek. I caught one small sunfish which I grilled over a little fire. Fortunately we'd brought sandwiches and a thermos of iced tea with us. Mary was so graceful, so nicely finished, a real pleasure to look at. I was thrilled to be with her, my first magic shiksa. She didn't like Tchaikovsky and she wasn't much interested when I wanted to read *The Rubaiyat of Omar Khayyam* to her but she seemed to like me and I thought she might be my girlfriend.

That summer day was all there was. A few days later when I asked her to go to the movies with me she turned me down. She said her parents didn't want her to go out with me. I asked her if it was because I was Jewish and she said yes. At school after that I'd see her in the halls with Karl Gunther and we'd both look away.

Thoughts of Mary Snyder took me to the big old wild cherry tree in our backyard and the books I used to read there as a child, sitting in its branches and eating sun-warmed cherries: three of my favourites were illustrated editions of *Robin Hood*, *The Arabian Nights* and *Treasure Island*. I still had them through high school but in 1959 my heart was broken when Jessica Williams dumped me for an older fellow who was in the Navy. As a broken-hearted lover I felt that I had entered man's estate. Life was hard, women were cruel; it was time to put childish things behind me, so I took those three books and burnt them in the backyard. I watched bits of charred pages flying and the smoke rising past the bare winter branches of the cherry tree with a lump in my throat and tears running down my face.

Jessica had been my first serious girlfriend as an adult, which is what I considered myself at seventeen when we began to go steady. In 1958 I cycled over a hundred miles to visit her in Wildwood, New Jersey where her parents had a seaside bungalow. They lived in Philadelphia and earlier that year I'd taken Jessica to a concert in Robin Hood Dell. The night was full of stars and the Philadelphia Orchestra played Tchaikovsky's *Romeo and Juliet Fantasy Overture*. The music swelled and my whole being swelled with it. I took her hand and squeezed it and she returned the pressure. First love!

Years later I wanted my three burnt books back, those editions and no others. They were, after all, a first love that never stopped being true to me even when their ashes were blowing in the wind. I haunted second-hand bookshops until I learned to use book searches and the Internet. I had no luck with *The Arabian Nights* because it was a cheap edition in which the illustrator had never been credited and I'd forgotten the publisher. I found the *Robin Hood* I wanted, illustrated by Edwin John Prittee, and only the other day I obtained from Abebooks my old *Treasure Island* with Louis Rhead's wonderful illustrations. I held it in my hands and the pictures and text sprang to life as juicy and soul-satisfying as when I had them in the cherry tree. The book fell open to the page with the *Hispaniola* nearing the island at night. THE MAN AT THE HELM WAS WATCHING THE LUFF OF THE SAIL, said the caption under Rhead's full-page pen-and-ink drawing in which Jim is about to get into the apple barrel, where he will hear:

Silver's voice, and before I heard a dozen words I would not have shown myself for all the world, but lay there, trembling and listening, in the extreme of fear and curiosity; for from those dozen words I understood that the lives of all the honest men aboard depended upon me alone.

No matter that Rhead drew a square-rigged ship when the *Hispaniola* was a schooner. Seeing that white moon in the pen-and-ink sky and the moonlit sea below, I could feel the warm wind filling the luff of that wrong sail. I turned from the picture to the text again and I had tears running down my face.

The Rubaiyat of Omar Khayyam was a teenage favourite that I never did think I outgrew; I still have the edition I wanted to read to Mary Snyder, the Fitzgerald translation, with an unforgettable drawing by Edmund J. Sullivan for each of the seventy-five quatrains of the first version. And I still know most of it by heart.

Recaptured childhood pleasures, however, were no help at present. Living alone was no longer good enough. Having opened myself to the possibility of not being alone, I now felt less than complete in Christabel's absence and anxious in the uncertainty of where we were with each other. I sensed that the things I didn't know about her were important. I also sensed that she was at some kind of hard place in herself. She was just as alone as I was and I didn't think she *should* be alone right now. The more I thought about it the more I wanted to talk to her. She'd said she was going to Honolulu and Maui but she hadn't given me any telephone numbers or the names of places where she could be reached.

25

CHRISTABEL ALDERTON

25 January 2003. And now a dead bat. Not just any bat but a rare one, an endangered species. I can imagine this bat – I'll call him Jim, he's from Maui. Hasn't been feeling all that great so he goes to his doctor for a check-up. Doc Bat says, 'What seems to be the problem?'

Jim says, 'Shortness of breath, chest pains, I pass out when I hang upside down, my echolocation is wonky, I have trouble taking off and I can't get any altitude.'

'Hmmm,' says the doc. Listens to Jim's heart, looks into his ears, opens and shuts his wings, says, 'Hmmm' again and shakes his head.

'What?' says Jim.

'I think,' says the doc, 'if there's anything you've always wanted to do but never got round to, now is the time to do it. If you can.'

'You mean . . . ?' says Jim.

'You got it,' says Doc Bat.

So Jim thinks he might as well try for Honolulu.

It's only a short hop but he's never found the time to go there and he'd like to see the bright lights and the action before he checks out. He takes off and he's flapping, flapping his way to Oahu. He's running out of petrol when he sees the lights and there's the airport with ALOHA in big letters on it. How he's over the Japanese garden and he echolocates me. 'My kind of human!' he squeaks. 'She's into this kind of thing.' And with that he drops dead in front of me.

OK, so Jim Bat got my number. Why not? I was probably broadcasting on all frequencies, ALDERTON'S MY NAME AND DEATH'S MY GAME. I felt sorry for Jim but I had other things to think about, like why I came here.

In 1993 when the grief in me was like something with hooks on it stuck in my throat, I spent a night at the Mini Hotel Sleep/Shower and the quietness and tranquillity of it calmed me down and helped me pull myself together. Now the Mini Hotel was gone but I thought I might find that old quietness in the gardens or the lounge in the middle of the night. It didn't happen. In my chair in the lounge I was tired but not sleepy; I was awake for a long time with my eyes feeling dry and sandy and I dozed off now and then with strange pictures in my head but no useful thoughts.

What I was feeling for Elias wasn't the kind of rush I had with Adam. How could it be with Elias and me both so much older? But when he held me that night while I cried I felt as if I'd come home after being gone for a long, long time. I'd been trying to keep my death life separate from the live life that Elias was part of. Why hadn't I told him about Django? If I told him about that I'd be inviting him into every part of my life and I wasn't sure he'd be safe there.

Henry turned up with a coffee for me. 'I thought you might be wakeful,' he said.

'Thank you. I was.' I said. 'Too much on my mind.'

'Remember,' said Henry. 'The bat chose you. You're special.'

26

ELIAS NEWMAN

29 January 2003. Jimmy Wicks's phone number was ex-directory but I remembered other band names. Howard Dent was not ex-directory and he gave me Jimmy's number. When I phoned I got Jimmy's ex-wife Tracy. She sounded as if the breakup had not been amicable and demanded to know why I wanted Jimmy's number. On the spur of the moment I said that he owed me money. 'That makes two of us,' she said. 'If you see that bastard, you tell him I've got friends who know where he lives.' She gave me a number, and when I dialled it the phone was answered by a man who sounded suspicious. He said Jimmy was out but he offered to take a message. I said who I was, told him I was calling about Christabel, said it was urgent, and left my number.

I wasn't very hopeful but he did actually phone me and said that he'd meet me at The Anchor & Hope in High Hill Ferry, Upper Clapton. With my *A to Z* I located the pub by the River Lea, opposite the

Walthamstow Marshes in E5. I took a taxi there and found him on a bench outside the pub, finishing a pint and looking at the river. The sky was grey and darkening, the wind was cold. Two Hassidic Jews all in black were on the path on the other side of the river, arguing about something as they walked. Their black gesticulations made the landscape seem more still, more bleak. A train clattered past the marshes to the bridge, grew larger, and was gone. Jimmy looked as if he'd drawn the short straw in a lifeboat where somebody was going to get eaten. He finished his pint, shook his head, and said, 'OK, here we are. Whatever it is you want to talk about, why couldn't we do it over the phone?'

'Let me get you another pint. What're you drinking?'

'London Pride.'

I got two, came back to the bench, and sat down. 'Cheers,' he said without much conviction.

'Cheers. I don't feel completely at ease with you, and I thought we could talk better face to face.'

'Why don't you feel at ease with me? Because you're screwing Christabel?'

'I don't feel at ease because I've noticed that you're not comfortable seeing me with her.'

'Are you or aren't you?'

'What?'

'Sleeping with her.'

'That's neither here nor there.'

'That means you are. So what's on your mind?'

'She's gone to Honolulu and Maui and she said it

was to do with the past. She seemed not in the best of spirits when she left. I was wondering . . .'

'You were wondering what I could tell you?'

'I feel awkward saying so, but yes, I was.'

'You feel awkward because if she wanted to tell you anything more than she did, she'd have done it, right?'

'OK, I felt kind of foolish coming to you but I'm worried about her.'

'Welcome to the club. Everybody that knows Christabel worries about her. My round.' He took our glasses and went inside. 'Thirsty work, talking about Christabel,' he said when he came back with our pints. 'Excuse me while I make a pit stop.' When he sat down again he said, 'Are you in love with her?'

'Yes.' So there it was, out of my own mouth. 'Are you?'

'Have been for years but she's never been interested in me.'

'But you've been married until recently.'

'So? That never stopped anyone from loving some-body else. You're not married?'

'That's right, I'm not.'

'Thinking of marrying Christabel?'

It was dark by then. The Anchor & Hope sent out its beams like a beacon for the weary traveller and the street lamp by our bench had come on while I sat here talking to Jimmy Wicks and saying what I'd never said to Christabel. A train chuntered past the marshes with its windows golden in the evening. It grew large, crossed the bridge and the reflecting river, and left a plume of silence behind as it disappeared. 'I'm super-stitious,' I said. 'I'd rather not say more about us just now, I don't want to jinx it. I know that something's troubling her but I don't know what it is. She said she's gone to Maui for a kind of remembrance day. Can you tell me anything about it?'

Jimmy sighed. 'Did you know she had a son?'

'No. Who was the father?'

'Guitarist with a German band, Adam Freund. He's dead now. So's the son.'

'What happened?'

'Light rig fell on Adam. That was in 1990. Three years later she went to Maui with her son – Django his name was and he was four years old. He fell off a cliff.'

'Jesus.'

'Jesus didn't save. She never got over it.'

'Understandably. Was she married to Django's father?

'He was married to somebody else. She's had a bad history with men.'

'What kind of bad?'

'There were three or four of them who met untimely deaths.'

'Are you saying that she had anything to do with that?'

'No, but I think it's always working on her.'

I nodded and so did he, then we both shook our heads and drank our London Pride in silence for a while. 'Any idea where she'd be staying on Maui?' I said.

'Probably the Pioneer Inn in Lahaina or Rudy Ka'uhane's place.'

'Who's Rudy Ka'uhane?'

'Just a friend, nothing romantic. He's a carpenter, made Django's coffin. The Pioneer Inn always knows where to reach him.'

'Thanks, it's really good of you to help me. You're a good man and I'm grateful to you.' I grabbed his hand and shook it. He seemed embarrassed.

'No use being a dog in the manger, is there. I'd really like to see her happy and I wish you luck.'

'I don't take anything for granted. I see you're ready for another pint.'

'They go down fast and they go through me fast. I'll be right back.'

I got a pint for him but none for me. When he came back I said, 'Are you thirstier than usual?'

'I am, actually.'

'Have to pee more than usual too?'

'That's right.'

'Might be a good idea to see your GP, get him to test your blood sugar.'

'You think I'm diabetic?'

'I think you should check your blood sugar.' I was remembering my father and the sweetness he couldn't metabolise. What a lot of blocked sweetness there is in the world!

27

CHRISTABEL ALDERTON

26 January 2003. Here I was then, with the night to get through and ten years ago on my mind. I'd thought January 1993 would be off-peak for holidaymakers but the Aloha Airlines flight was full, many of them hoping to see whales. 'I'd like to swim with them,' said a boy across the aisle to his girlfriend.

'I don't think they let you do that unless you're David Attenborough,' she said.

Django was craning his neck to see out of the window. 'Are there sharks down there?' he said.

'All kinds of things,' I said. Such a deep dark blue, the water below us, then a fringe of white surf as Kahului Airport came into view back in 1993. The palm trees were moving a little as if they didn't care one way or the other. It was a dull day and those trees put a jungly smell in my mind.

Some of the arrivals were being greeted with leis, some not. Bert Gresham had been to Maui and he had arranged for Rudy Ka'uhane to meet us. Rudy was holding a placard that said ALOHA CHRISTABEL & DJANGO in large capitals. I was startled to see Django's name like that, it was almost as if he'd grown up and gone away. He was quite pleased with it because he could already read his name. 'Aloha,' said Rudy, and he hung leis around our necks. Then he explained the *honi* greeting and did it with Django and me just as I did it with Henry Panawae this night ten years later. The pink flowers of our leis looked edible and they smelled like youth and first love, which seemed a little shocking since they and I had only just met. 'Plumeria,' said Rudy. 'My wife grows them at our place. Those are some of our leis that the kids are hanging on people now.'

'But not on everybody,' I said.

'Some of them are ordered before the flight, some people buy them here, others don't bother with them.' A very large brown man, Rudy. He was wearing shorts and a T-shirt and his arms and legs were like tree trunks. He took our cases and led the way to his car, and when we stepped outside the jungly smell I'd had in my mind was the real smell of the place. With a little petrol added.

Django said, 'This is far away.'

'Yes,' I said, 'it is.'

'Far-away trees.' he said.

'Palm trees,' I said. The sun had come out and it printed the shadows of the palms on the ground with every frond and the spaces between sharp and clear and black.

'Does God see everything?' said Django.

'What makes you ask that?' I said.

'The shadows.'

'Well,' I said, 'He sees what He wants to see. Sometimes He looks away.'

Django nodded. We'd never talked about God, he must have picked it up in playgroup.

'God is somebody who looks away most of the time,' said Rudy to me. 'He sure was looking away when the Americans hijacked these islands.'

'What do you mean?' I said.

'You don't know what I'm talking about, they don't have it in white history books?'

'Rudy,' I said, 'I'm a singer with a rock band and I don't read a whole lot of history.'

'OK. In 1900 Hawaii became a US territory. It was illegally annexed and everything since then, statehood and the rest of it, is illegal. I better not get started on this. Here's my car.' His Land Rover looked as if it had a lot of mileage on it and not much of it on roads. A hand-lettered bumper sticker said KOKO AND NO UKE.

'What's *koko*?' I said.

'Hawaiian blood. Don't matter if you got a lot or a little, you Hawaiian and your land been took from you. So let's get it back.'

Django and I were both knackered from all those hours of travel and Rudy was making me uncomfortable. 'Could we perhaps put history and politics aside for now?' I said. 'We're only here for the whales.'

'What's *uke*?' said Django.

'Ukelele,' said Rudy. He mimed strumming one. 'I don't got no *uke* for playin' on da beach at Waikiki.'

Django let that pass. 'I like this car,' he said.

'Her name is Lucille,' said Rudy.

'Like B. B. King's guitar?' I said.

'You got it. She da kine good old girl.'

'You da kine good old man?' said Django.

'That's me,' said Rudy. 'You da kine smart kid, brah.'

'When I'm big I'll have a Lucille,' said Django.

'She da one,' said Rudy. 'You da kine man she like.'

'What's *da kine*?' I said.

'It's just only a kind of talk we do here sometimes,' said Rudy. He loaded our luggage and us into Lucille and off we went with a roar and various rattles. 'I'll take you to the Pioneer Inn now,' he said. 'You'll want to get some rest, have a look around Lahaina. Tomorrow I'll show you the Iao Needle, next day you do a whale-watching cruise.'

'What's the Iao Needle?' said Django.

'It's a big rock in Iao Valley State Park – it's something you should see before we go anywhere else.'

'How come?' said Django.

'You'll see when we're there,' said Rudy.

'When we go whale-watching,' I said, 'we don't want to do it from a boat.'

'Why not?' said Rudy.

'I've been having bad dreams about water.'

147

'No problem, I can show you where to watch from shore. Tomorrow I'll bring you something to keep away bad dreams.'

There was singing on Lucille's radio but the engine noise was drowning it out until Rudy pulled over and stopped. Then we could hear, in Hawaiian at first, a vocalist with very lush backing and a voice that was like the voice of oceans and islands coming on the wind from far away. The refrain was in English:

> Cry for the gods, cry for the people,
> Cry for the land that was taken away,
> And then yet you'll find Hawai'i.

'Who is that?' I asked Rudy.

'IZ,' said Rudy. 'Israel Kamakawiwo'ole.'

'So much loss in the words and in his voice!'

'Loss is the only game in town,' said Rudy. 'Loss is the main action of this world. Anybody says different don't know what's what.'

Lucille started off again and nobody said anything for a while. We were on the Kuihelani Highway heading down to the coast where we turned into the highway to Lahaina. We had the sea to our left and the mountains to the right but I was too tired to take much in and that song had filled me with sadness. Django had fallen asleep in my lap clutching his cloth crocodile.

It's 2003 as I write this about 1993. I know I'm getting the conversations right but some of my comments can't help being from now rather than ten years ago. Lahaina used to be a whalers' town. Now it was selling itself as a place that used to be a whalers' town. A while back a movie was made that starred Spencer Tracy and Frank Sinatra, *The Devil at Four O'Clock*. This island played the part of Talua, a non-existent movie island. Lahaina and the Pioneer Inn were featured as somewhere else and there was still a poster to prove that it happened.

In the early nineteenth century (some local history here that I picked up) Lahaina became known as the whaling capital of the Pacific. It was a sailors' town where women and drink and violence were plentiful. There was more violence in the 1820s when the missionaries came to town, not to give instruction in the missionary position but to fight sin. Sin fought back, and the sailors even fired their cannon at the mission. Eventually the local chiefs restored order, and seamen who didn't return to their ships at sundown were imprisoned. By 1901, when the Pioneer Inn opened, Lahaina was pretty well civilised. The house rules from that year include:

YOU MUST PAY YOU RENT IN ADVANCE.
YOU MUST NOT LET YOU ROOM GO ONE
  DAY BACK.
WOMEN IS NOT ALLOW IN YOU ROOM.
IF YOU WET OR BURN YOU BED YOU GOING
  OUT.
YOU ARE NOT ALLOW TO GIVE YOU BED TO
  YOU FREAND.
ONLY ON SUNDAY YOU CAN SLEEP ALL DAY.

The Pioneer Inn was meant to look like an old plantation house, I was told. Sugar was still big business; the cane was burned in the Pioneer Mill whose stack overlooked the town. The inn was a very wide building with a red roof and a veranda across the whole front of it at the second level. A very shipshape-looking place. The building was blue-grey with white posts and railings, window frames and doors. From our veranda we looked out on banyan trees and Front Street and over the water to blue mountains that were like mountains in a dream. I was seeing them for the first time but they seemed half remembered, half forgotten. I thought there might be words in my mind but when I opened my mouth nothing came.

The room was plain but good: white walls and a handsome bed with a watercolour over it of a little red-roofed house among palm trees – an original painting, not a print. The lamp on the bedside table had a lathe-turned base of dark polished wood which matched the bedposts. There was a cot for Django on which he went back to sleep immediately. I've known a lot of hotel rooms in my time. It's always as if a self has gone ahead to wait for you in the room; maybe a self you didn't know you had that day: a happy self or a sad one, whatever. You walk into the room and it says, 'Hi. This is how we are today.' But I wasn't sure where I was and I couldn't remember why I'd wanted so much to watch whales. In my ignorance I'd thought of Maui just as a place where you went to enjoy yourself but after listening to Rudy and that song I felt that these islands really didn't want me and Django.

We both had a good kip, then went out past the little lighthouse to the harbour where the whalers used to anchor. There was a square-rigged ship there, the *Carthaginian*. This ship also starred in a movie, *Hawaii*, for which it was converted from a Baltic cargo schooner to its present incarnation. As far as I could make out it never had been a whaler, although now it housed a whaling museum. Django wanted to see it so we went aboard. There was the skeleton of a whale that you could walk through but Django wouldn't. 'It doesn't want us here,' he said. The harpoons and lances upset him, as well as the blubber knives and try pots. 'This is a bad place,' he said, and we left.

The other vessels in the harbour were expensive sailing boats, cabin cruisers and sport-fishermen and the water sparkled with dollar signs. There were T-shirts with whales on them in the shops and the *Lahaina News* advertised a Slack Key Guitar Festival. Still, it was charming and lively, full of places where you could spend time and money. I mustn't let the jaded me of 2003 get in the way. I bought Django a T-shirt with a humpback whale on it and a baseball cap that said MAUI.

Later we went to the I'O nearby in Front Street for a candlelit dinner outside under the trees. For starters we had steamed wontons filled with 'roasted peppers, mushrooms, spinach, macadamia nuts and silken tofu over a fragrant tomato coulis with a creamy basil yogurt purée'. The list of ingredients with its adjectives was so colourful that I took a menu away with me for a souvenir. We shared a Maui steak after that and finished up with pineapple ice cream. Front Street was full of tourists enjoying their evening as we went back to the Pioneer Inn. Some of them were singing.

When Django was asleep I went out on to the veranda. The sky had cleared and there was a little sliver of crescent moon. I stood there looking at the stars until I found the Plough. That's all right then, I thought. This is home too. But I didn't quite believe it.

28

ELIAS NEWMAN

30 January 2003. It was as if the ocean were sending up to me songs of my childhood. One of the songs we sang in Morning Exercises was 'My Faith Looks Up to Thee':

> My faith looks up to thee,
> Thou lamb of Calvary,
> Saviour divine!
> Now hear me while I pray,
> take all my guilt away,
> O let me from this day
> be wholly thine!

I didn't have any Christian guilt but the hymn had a good sound to it and I joined in with a will. The verse I liked best was the last one. It accorded well with the darkness that was in me even then:

When ends life's transient dream,
when death's cold sullen stream
shall o'er me roll;
blest Saviour, then in love,
fear and distrust remove;
O bear me safe above,
a ransomed soul!

I had no idea of a Saviour and ransomed souls but death's cold sullen stream rang true for me. Now I was reflecting that we are all of us little chips of life borne on death's cold sullen stream to the ocean of nothingness. No more anything. I shook myself to shake off those thoughts; I didn't want them to connect with my thoughts of Christabel.

'Somebody walk over your grave?' said the woman next to me. American. Fat, middle-aged.

'They do it all the time,' I said.

'You get used to it,' she said. 'Try Jack Daniel's.'

'Have they got it on the drinks trolley?' I said.

'Johnny Walker will do the job too,' she said. 'I just happen to like sour mash when they start walking.'

'Who?'

'Over my grave. Ex-husbands. Worthless bastards.'

'How many?'

'A fifth will usually last me two days, sometimes not.'

'I meant husbands, not drinks.'

'Four.'

'Why so many?'

'Kept trying to get it right, never did.'

'You must have loved them, at least in the beginning?'

She suddenly took on a sharper focus and her face zoomed to a close-up. She fixed me with a penetrating glance and said, 'What's love? Can you tell me?'

'I don't think it's something that can be defined.'

'I didn't think you could. I'm going to watch a movie now.'

Left to myself I didn't try to define love. I had heard myself say that I was in love with Christabel and I believed it without understanding it. Sometimes late at night I watch major league baseball on TV. Abstractly, without caring who's playing. I enjoy the dramatic moments, as in bottom of the ninth and the team I'm rooting for trying to hold on to a one-run lead with the other team at bat and two outs. The pitcher (whoever he is) looks to the catcher, waves off the sign, goes into his wind-up. Here's the pitch, a low fast ball but not fast enough. The batter (leading the league in RBIs this season) connects and, Wow! There it goes, going, going . . . The centre fielder races back, back, back and up the wall, up, up, yes! He's got it! What a catch. OK, so love hadn't escaped me. But that was just my end of it. Did Christabel love me? She liked my company and was willing to go to bed with me but lots of people do that without being in love. Her history wasn't the usual thing. Woody Guthrie came to mind with his songs about hard travelling down various roads. I'd sung those songs to myself at one time and another; maybe Christabel had too – life is full of rough roads. By now probably anything with a man looked like hard travelling to her. Sometimes she felt like a bad-luck carrier, she'd said. For me the worst luck would be to lose her, and while the plane seemed perfectly still high above the ocean I leant forward in the roaring recycled silence, straining towards her, afraid that she couldn't love me, that I couldn't hold her, that she'd slip through my fingers and be lost. I went back to the galley and one of the flight attendants said, 'Hi. What can we do for you?' A pretty young woman with a knowing air and a figure that gladdened the eye.

'I know this isn't drinks time,' I said, 'but do you think I could have two of those little bottles of Johnny Walker?'

'Did you bring a note from your mother?' she said.

'Actually you might say it's for medicinal purposes. I'm a doctor.'

'OK,' she said. 'I trust you. I'll even pour it into a glass for you. Straight up?'

'Neat,' I said. 'No ice, no water.'

'You got it, Doc. Go back to your seat and I'll bring it to you.'

'Thank you, I feel better already. You're very kind.'

'What are flight attendants for?' she said with a compassionate smile.

An answer almost leapt to my lips but I limited myself to another smile. When she brought me the whisky she said, 'There you go, Doc. If symptoms persist buzz me.'

'You got it,' I said. It was a pleasure to watch her walk away. With scotch in hand I went back to my anxiety in an easier state of mind.

I was halfway through my drink when suddenly all ease left me and I saw Christabel Alderton climbing the stairs of the old mission in *Vertigo*. 'No,' I said. 'Please no.'

The woman beside me had on her headphones and I don't think she heard me. I finished the whisky and resumed my forward lean. Although my seat was on the aisle I kept my eye on the window. There was no sign of Bat Air.

29

RITA HENDERSON

30 January 2003. If I had an electric eye and a buzzer in the back of my skirt there'd be a lot of noise following me around. Of course there isn't room for an electric eye and a buzzer. I think it's nice when older men take an interest and this one certainly did. When they have good manners like that doctor I think it might make a nice change sometime from the usual guys I go with. Not that pilots are all that young. I like a little refinement in a man. And that's what I mostly get: very damn little. Oh well, some day my prince will come. But not prematurely, I hope.

The doctor really did seem troubled when he asked for the scotch. I wonder what he was troubled about. I'm twenty-eight and I'd guess he was in his late fifties. When I'm twice as old as I am now, what's it going to be like? Rafe Simmonds, the pilot on our last flight to HNL, said to me during our layover,

'Now it takes me all night to do what I used to do all night.'

'I like a man who takes his time,' I said. Well, what else could I say?

30

FLORENCE JASPER

26 January 2003. That guy next to me in the plane had some kind of trouble on his mind. Sex, money, death? Maybe all three. You never know what's going on inside another person. My No. 4, Herb Jasper, on Tuesday he was OK, no problems. On Wednesday he put the muzzle of his 12-gauge in his mouth and blew his head off. You just never know.

31

ANNELIESE NEWMAN

26 January 2003. Here am I, not yet dead. There are no productions of *Traviata* with Violetta and Alfredo in their nineties. Who would pay money to see and hear it? Especially the ending. 'Die already!' the audience would shout. One only cares about Violetta because she is young and beautiful. And Schubert, he wrote '*Der Tod und das Mädchen*' but he did not follow this with '*Der Tod und die Greisin*', 'Death and the Old Woman'. *Der Tod* himself is bored with old women, how could he not be?

I still have my teeth, my eyes, my hearing and my mind. In me is the pretty girl I was, *das Mädchen* Anneliese Linde. If I close my eyes I see the sky reflected in the Weser and I hear the wind in the birches and smell the grasses warm from the sun. I am ready to go back there for ever. 'Here am I,' I say. But *der Tod* sees not the pretty girl and passes me by.

32

CHRISTABEL ALDERTON

27 January 2003. Back in 1993 after our first night in the Pioneer Inn I woke up feeling not all that keen for a visit to Iao Valley State Park but Rudy seemed to think it was important and I didn't want to spoil the day for Django.

We had breakfast and I wouldn't have minded a few more cups of coffee but here was Rudy bright and early. Django said, 'We going in Lucille?' He had Crocodile with him and he was ready for action.

'Partly,' said Rudy, 'and partly we goin' be luggin' it, brah.'

'OK,' said Django, 'les' do it, Uncle.'

'How come you called me Uncle?'

'I don't know. Can you be my uncle?'

'You got it, Nephew,' said Rudy, and scooped him up and carried him off to the Land Rover. Django hadn't ever wanted any of the guys in the band to be his uncle.

Lucille started off with her usual roar and we were

off. The day was grey and cloudy. 'How far is it?' I asked Rudy.

'About twenty miles, maybe little more. We gotta go down the coast to Maalaea Harbor then up Kahekili Highway to the Iao Valley. Keiko packed some sandwiches in case we get hungry while we're out.'

'Who's Keiko?' said Django.

'My wife,' said Rudy. 'She's Japanese.'

'Could I have a sandwich now?' said Django. He was never good at waiting for picnics. I was hungry too and so was Rudy so we finished the sandwiches and a flask of tea after we'd been on the road less than a quarter of an hour.

'Are we going to see whales?' said Django.

'Iao Needle today, whales tomorrow,' said Rudy.

We went down the coast with the sea to our right and the mountains to our left. Yesterday the mountains I'd seen from the veranda had looked mystical but these didn't. I knew the islands were volcanic, risen out of the sea millions of years ago; looking at these mountains today, I didn't like the idea of them bursting up out of the sea as if something down there had heaved them off its back. I thought of the mountains of experience in me and I shook my head to make my thoughts go away while Lucille shook, rattled and snarled as the Kahekili Highway began to climb a little and Rudy changed gears.

It was cool but not cold as we turned off for the valley. When we entered the park it grew cooler as the road took us among the fresh-smelling trees. We passed a shrine in which stood a madonna hung with leis. In front of her were three figures which I took to be wise men, also a couple of animals, sheep perhaps. Rudy didn't stop. '*Haole*,' he muttered.

'*Haole* is Christmas?' said Django.

Rudy shook his head. '*Haole* is foreigners. Those wonderful people who brought us Christianity, syphilis, and gonorrhoea.'

'What are syphilis and gonorrhoea?' said Django.

'Diseases,' I said. To Rudy I said, 'Don't you think this might be a little heavy for a four-year-old? And Django and I are foreigners.'

'Sorry,' said Rudy. 'I was talking about foreigners way back. Now I'll get off my soapbox for the rest of the day.'

Rudy parked the car and we walked up a paved pathway beside a stream. I'd put on a pair of trainers and was quite comfortable. The smell and sound of the water and the smell of the trees were refreshing. The air seemed full of presences.

'What happened here?' said Django.

'How do you know something happened?' said Rudy.

'I can feel it,' said Django. 'Are there ghostes all around us?' He always pronounced 'ghosts' with two syllables.

'I can feel it too,' I said. 'What is it?'

'*Mana*,' said Rudy. 'Spiritual power. In 1790 there was a big battle when King Kamehamea and his army wiped out the Maui warriors. What you're feeling is the power of all those spirits. I've brought people here who couldn't feel anything. I thought you would and I'm glad you did.'

'A kind of test, was it?' I said.

'Everything is,' said Rudy.

'Your guys lost the battle?' said Django to Rudy.

'Don't matter,' said Rudy. 'Kamehamea was trying to unify these islands.'

'Did he?' I said.

'Yes, but it took him almost thirty years.'

'Who's king now?' said Django.

'Nobody,' said Rudy.

The walk was long enough to tire Django after a while, and Rudy took him on his shoulders. Eventually we came to a sign that said IAO NEEDLE ELEV. 2250 FT. And there it was sticking up beyond the trees, not so much a needle as an irregular cone of darkness. Beyond it the valley was filled with cloud. The air was wet and the cold and rushing water of the stream sent up spray as it went splashing and tumbling and burbling over the rocks. The water was shouting as if it was the under-voice of the Iao Needle.

'Talking,' said Django.

'Who?' said Rudy.

Django pointed to the Needle.

'What's it saying?' said Rudy.

'No words.'

'That rock could tell a lot of stories if it wanted to,' said Rudy. 'Maybe that's what it's doing in Needletalk.'

'I can't see his face,' said Django.

'Whose face?' I said.

Again he pointed to the Needle.

'If we go up on the bridge we can see it from a different angle,' said Rudy. So we went up on the bridge. There was a roofed shelter at one end and we looked at the Needle from there. This time I could see that it was covered with green foliage or mosses.

'Still no face,' said Django.

'I've never seen a face myself,' said Rudy.

'Whichever way I look, he turns his back,' said Django.

'Some rocks are like that,' said Rudy. 'My house is closer than the Pioneer Inn, so if it's OK with you we'll go there and you can rest up, then I'll cook you a real Hawaiian dinner.'

33

ELIAS NEWMAN

26 January 2003. You never know where you're going to be attacked by a metaphor or run over by a paradigm. In the Tom Bradley International Terminal in Los Angeles there's a sort of pinball machine stood up on legs like a lecturer's blackboard. It's a ball-dropping machine. A conveyor on one side picks up balls that have rolled on to it from the channels they've dropped into. It carries the balls up to the top and drops them on to a Heath Robinson arrangement of such channels. There are various other parts that do things but the main action is ball-dropping. Not always the same because of random elements that vary the effects and causes. The machine is worn and doesn't always pick the balls up. There are no plungers to work, you have no way of controlling what it does. The machine is just what it is and it does its own thing imperfectly in a variety of ways while making noises that satirise pinball machines. A man joined me while I was pondering this. He slapped the glass hard a couple of

times, cursed and moved on while the machine made derisory noises. I stood there for a long time as other hopeful punters failed in their efforts. There was a signature on the thing: Rhoads '96. A deep one, Mr Rhoads.

Before I left St Eustace I looked in on Abraham Selby. I have never forgotten Professor Ernst's words about the doctor–patient relationship (I notice that I don't say patient–doctor. There are traditional orders of words: men and women; Adam and Eve; steak and kidney; plus and minus; willy-nilly. Nobody says nilly-willy.) I have never been a verticalist. Abraham Selby, although horizontal in his bed, was in himself as vertical as I was. Perhaps even a little more so sometimes.

On this morning there he was with his lachrymose leg propped up as always and his copy of *The Times* in hand. 'Sometimes there's good news when you least expect it,' he said.

'So tell me,' I said.

'Have a look.' He folded the paper as necessary and passed it to me. I'd been too busy booking my flight to read my copy at home. There was a one-column item with a colour photograph of an upside-down bottle of Heinz tomato ketchup sporting a right-side-up label. SAUCE FLIPS TO GO WITH THE FLOW was the headline.

[Heinz] has spent millions of pounds and three years on research to come up with an upside-down bottle with a cap and valve in its bottom. It is a solution that customers hit upon years ago – seven out of ten say they balance their sauce bottles on their tops.

'How's that grab you?' said Selby.

'It's definitely good news,' I said.

'Things go on the same year after year,' said Selby, 'then all at once they get turned around. Pay attention,' he said to his leg. To me he said, 'Think about it.'

I did.

34

CHRISTABEL ALDERTON

27 January 2003. Rudy's house was in Hamakua Poko, on high ground overlooking a gulch. It was surrounded by trees except on the side that looked towards the sea. I was expecting something recognisably Hawaiian but this was a very modern structure with solar panels on the roof, a lot of glass and a cantilevered deck. 'Built it myself,' said Rudy. 'Koa wood. This wood has Hawaiian soul, it's the mother and father wood. They used to make sailing canoes from it. I stand on that deck and look out to sea where it's full of sport-fishermen and yachts now and I see the ghosts of those canoes with the crab-claw sails. Out they go over the horizon into never-never. All gone with the *mana* that was in them. You don't have to say anything.'

'Never-never,' said Django. He liked the sound of it.

Rudy named the trees for me but only a few of the names stuck in my memory: banana, mango, bread-fruit, macadamia nut and tamarind. There were flowers everywhere, some of them plumeria, like the leis we'd been given. There was a tree that stood apart from the others; there were beautiful purple blossoms on it. I admit that I cry easily and I don't always know why.

'Why are you crying?' said Rudy.

'No reason,' I said. 'It's just the purple. What is this tree?'

'Jacaranda. It's Esperanza's tree.'

'Who's Esperanza?'

'Our daughter. She's buried here.'

'How old was she?'

'She was stillborn.'

'What's stillborn?' said Django.

'Born dead,' said Rudy.

Django didn't say anything for a few moments, then, 'Did God look away?'

Oh dear, I thought. I'd been hoping he'd inherit my atheism.

'Yes,' said Rudy. 'He looked away.'

'Why?' said Django.

'Because He's crazy,' said Rudy.

Again there was a little quiet space. Then Django said, 'But He made the world.'

'That proves it,' said Rudy. He took us to the greenhouse which was close by, set among trees. It was big and professional-looking.

'Did you build this too?' said Django.

'Yes. Keiko designed it and I built it.' He opened the door and we walked into a whole bright world of flowers and their fragrances. Keiko had been working, and she took off her gloves as she came to meet us. She was wearing shorts and a T-shirt but when she smiled it was like a silk fan opening with a Japanese court lady from another century painted on it. She picked up two leis with yellow flowers and hung them round our necks. 'Aloha,' she said, and did the *honi* greeting with Django and me. 'These are your second greeting on your first visit. These kuala-mani plumeria are saying that you are twice welcome in our house.'

'Thank you,' I said. 'This is for you.' I gave her a pair of very delicate enamelled violet-flower earrings from the thirties with a matching necklace. She put them on straightaway and I'd made the right choice.

'I've never had violets before,' she said, and kissed me.

'This is for you,' said Django to Rudy, and gave him one of the more complex Swiss army knives.

'*Mahalo*,' said Rudy to Django. 'I keep this with me always and think of you.'

'Plumeria,' said Django as he looked down at his lei.

'There are twenty-five different kinds of plumeria,' said Keiko. It's the most popular flower for leis. We don't grow them in here but they're all over the place outside. And as you see, we have a few other things as well. This rose here is lokelani, it's the official flower of this island. In other places it's called a damask rose.' It was a juicy-looking rose with a lovely pink colour and a smell that made you feel like waltzing.

'Yes,' said Keiko when she saw my feet moving, 'it dances.' She showed us orchids, heliconia, hibiscus, jasmines, gardenias and many more with names I don't remember. I'm good with songs but not with trees and flowers.

Rudy had been busy in the kitchen while we were doing the greenhouse tour. We'd be having lunch in the large room with sliding glass doors that opened on to the deck. It was a bright room and it was made brighter by the flowers in it. The doors were open and a pleasant breeze stirred them and their fragrances. When Django saw the table he said to Rudy, 'You made this too.'

'Right,' said Rudi. Although the table was flat it tapered to a point at both ends and the benches on either side were attached to it like outriggers on a canoe.

'Koa?' said Django.

'What else?' said Rudy.

In a corner of the room stood a screen, the kind you see women changing behind in films. All three panels were completely covered with pressed flowers under clear plastic. They were like beautiful ghosts caught in mid-flight; their ghost-colours are with me still, flower-thoughts and flower-memories. I recognised plumeria, jacaranda, hibiscus, lokelani and one or two more but when I asked Keiko for the names of the others she shook her head. 'Don't think names,' she said, 'just think flowers.' I was going to ask if I could take a picture of the screen but then I decided not to. At home I have stacks of photographs of things I wanted to remember but when I try to recall those scenes and people what my mind gives me are the photos. Now, with no photo and no list of names I see that screen with its ghosts and I hear Django saying to Keiko, 'What's behind it?'

'Ancestors,' she said, and folded back a panel to show him the little shrine with its framed photographs of people with serious faces.

'Dead?' said Django.

'Yes.'

He put his hands together and bowed as he'd seen it done in films and Keiko closed the screen and kissed him.

While Rudy was charcoal-grilling some of the thirty-five-pound fish he'd caught early that morning (*ono* was its name) we had sashimi with two kinds of dip, breadfruit chips and breadfruit fritters, and Steinlager beer. For Django there was fresh limeade and lemonade. Rudy seasoned the fish with black pepper, garlic butter and fresh-squeezed lime and it made me feel that everything I'd eaten before today hadn't been real food. Django liked it too.

'He eats like a grown-up,' said Keiko.

'Better than some,' I said. 'New things are no problem for him.'

By the time Rudy laid out a big platter of fruit Django's eyes were closing. 'Crocodile?' he said.

'I'd have to send out for that,' said Rudy.

I took Crocodile out of my bag and gave it to Django

and he was asleep before his head hit the pillow for his afternoon nap in one of the guest rooms.

'That's one hell of a kid you got there,' said Rudy.

'Thank you,' I said. 'If he was on the shelf in a kid store he's probably the one I'd take home.'

'Is he like his father?' said Keiko. 'I ask because he seems to have more in him than most kids.'

'More what?' I said.

'Soul?'

Whenever I thought of Adam I could see him clearly, his face in the rosy lamplight and I could hear 'Nuages'. And then what he said when I asked for his address and phone number. 'When Django grows up I don't think he'll cheat on his wife or anybody else,' I said. Not an appropriate response but that's what came out of my mouth.

'I'm sorry,' said Keiko. 'I ought not to have intruded into your past.'

'That's all right,' I said. 'My past itself is the intruder. I tell myself not to look back but it's always in front of me.'

'We know something about that,' said Rudy. 'The only thing is to keep busy. Keiko runs our lei business and I do guiding, carpentry, anything that comes along.'

'Plus *koko and no uke*,' said Keiko.

'We got to repossess our country,' said Rudy. 'Hawaii can't go on being just a tourist attraction full of Uncle Toms handing out leis and doing the hula and luaus. We're not part of the United States, we have a culture and a history of our own. We come from a people who made big double canoes with crab-claw sails for voyaging thousands of miles. With their hands they carved the canoes and wove the sails and took their chances on the open sea. They didn't know what was over the horizon and they had no compass and no maps to show the way to the new islands they were looking for.'

'Where did they come from?' I said.

'First from Samoa to the Marquesas, then the Marquesas to here,' said Rudy.

'Why couldn't they stay where they were?'

'Because they wanted to see what was over the horizon,' said Rudy. 'I think Django'll do the same when he's grown.'

'How did they find Hawaii?' I asked.

'They watched waves and currents, wind and stars,' said Rudy. 'They watched birds and they scanned the sky for the loom of islands that were out of sight and they found them. They found Hawaii and made it our home but after the whites took over there was a time when even our language was banned, along with the hula, not the pretty one for tourists but the real one that told our history. We're better than the people who took this country from us.'

'Take it easy,' said Keiko. 'You're among friends. You don't have to be the big *kahuna* with us.'

'OK,' said Rudy. 'I'm taking it easy.'

Probably nobody has an easy life, I thought. We sat there looking out at the sky getting dark over the sea.

When it was time to go Keiko gave me a corked bottle full of some muddy liquid. 'Drink about half a cup of this before you go to bed,' she said. 'I made it for you fresh. It will give you a good night's sleep.'

'What is it?' I said.

'It's kava, made from the roots of the pepper plant.'

'Thank you,' I said. 'I'll try it.'

As we went down the Kuihelani Highway to the coast and than back to Lahaina the road kept coming towards us in the headlights and everything felt like noplace.

'Maybe there are whales out there in the dark,' said Django.

That night, long after Django had been put to bed, I stood on the veranda and looked up at the sky. There was a heavy overcast; I couldn't see the moon and I couldn't see the Plough and home wasn't where I was.

35

ELIAS NEWMAN

30 January 2003. Soon I'd be in Honolulu where I'd
get a flight to Maui. Now that I knew about Django's
death I was very uneasy about this 'rememberance day'
that Christabel had said was the purpose of her trip.
Such a strange woman – so full of life and so pre-
occupied with death.

I can never get used to the passage of the self through
time and space and the passage of time and space
through the self. The years in me surged up like acid
reflux to mingle with the travel hours I was trying to
digest while the miles lay like a lump in my stomach
and half-forgotten songs spun in my head: 'The stars
shine above you,/ Yet linger awhile;/ They whisper "I
love you,"/ So linger awhile . . .' Along with 'The
Spanish Cavalier', 'Juanita', 'Herr Oluf' and other
greatest hits.

So what was all this about, this late-blooming love?
Why not slide gently and smoothly into old age
without all this aggravation? 'Don't be stupid,' I said

to myself. 'It happened and you don't have a choice. And this kind of aggravation is what makes you not dead. Be thankful for it.'

'OK,' I said, 'I'm thankful.' I leant forward in my seat and cursed the slowness of the plane.

36

JIMMY WICKS

27 January 2003. When you think of it, making songs and performing them is a strange thing to do. Sometimes when I'm watching other bands on TV I turn off the sound and there are these guys working up a sweat and jumping around and moving their mouths and they look pretty stupid. This evening I was standing outside The Anchor & Hope looking at the river and watching a cabin cruiser, *Blue Guitar*, go by when a train went over the bridge. Did I hear the boat and the train? I wasn't sure. Was the sound turned off just for a moment?

37

CHRISTABEL ALDERTON

30 January 2003. Still doing my remembering of 1993. It's like a hair shirt. On the morning of our second full day on Maui, Django and I had an early breakfast at the Pioneer Inn and got ready to be picked up by Rudy. The weather was cool and cloudy and I didn't particularly feel like watching for whales although that was the whole purpose of the trip. I'd have been quite happy to have a second breakfast somewhere on Front Street and linger over coffee. I'd drunk the kava before going to bed. It was bitter and it made my mouth and throat numb after a couple of minutes but then the warmth of it spread through me and I was off into a deep sleep. I had bad dreams that I couldn't remember and I woke up with a heavy head and a bad taste in my mouth and here was Rudy. 'Have a good night?' he said.

'The kava helped me sleep all right,' I said. 'Now I'd like to wake up. I've got what feels like a hang-over.'

'You have to be eighteen to order kava in a kava bar,' said Rudy. 'You *can* feel it the next morning if you're not as strong as you might be.'

'Now you tell me.'

'Whales today?' said Rudy. Lucille was panting and growling and ready to roll.

'Is there a place with a good view of the action and not too many other tourists?' I said.

'We could go up the coast and around to Kahakuloa Head,' said Rudy. 'There are good lookouts along the cliffs and it's a nice drive.'

'OK,' I said, 'let's do that.' And off we went, with the sea to our left looking cold and heavy.

'Kahakuloa Head,' said Django. He liked the sound of it. 'Has it got a face?'

'No,' said Rudy. 'It isn't that kind of a head. It's just a great big rock sticking up out of the water.'

'Kahakuloa Head,' said Django again. 'No face. No eyes.'

'Here's Kaanapali,' said Rudy. He stopped Lucille and pulled over to the side. 'See the train?' He pointed to the right where a Disneyland kind of old-fashioned steam train was huffing and puffing, all red and black and brass.

'Hooeee!' echoed Django as it blew its whistle.

'A-N-A-K-A,' he said, reading off the gold letters on the side of the red cab.

'*Anaka* must be the name of the engine,' I said. LK & P RR were the gold letters on the black tender. Django couldn't do anything with the ampersand.

'That's what used to be the old sugar train, the Lahaina–Kaanapali and Pacific Railroad,' said Rudy. 'Look down there to your left at that black rock that juts out into the water.' We looked. There was a white bird with black markings and long black tail streamers wheeling over it.

'It's sacred, that rock,' said Rudy. 'Kekaa is its name. That's where Maui souls used to jump off into the spirit world.'

'That bird down there, is it a soul?' said Django.

'That's a tropic-bird,' said Rudy. 'Maybe it's a soul, I don't know.'

'You said they used to jump off there,' said Django. 'Don't they do it any more?'

'I don't know,' said Rudy. 'Maybe they do.'

'Some of them must come from far away,' said Django. 'So they have to fly there?'

'OK,' said Rudy. 'That makes sense.'

'So why do they need to jump off a rock?' said Django. 'Why don't they just fly straight into the spirit world?'

'You got me there,' said Rudy.

'Maybe the black rock is a door to the spirit world,' said Django. 'That's why they have to come there.'

'That's the best explanation I've heard so far,' said Rudy.

Ten years ago and I remember every word. We went up along the coast through Kapalua. 'This is where they grow golf, hotels and pineapples,' said Rudy.

'What's golf?' said Django.

183

'People hitting a little white ball with fancy clubs,' said Rudy.

'How can they grow golf and hotels?' said Django.

'They plant money and the golf and the hotels spring up,' said Rudy.

'Where do they get the money?' said Django.

'From tourists,' said Rudy.

'Like me and Mum?' said Django.

Rudy looked at me and wiped imaginary sweat from his brow.

'Don't look at me,' I said to him. 'You started it with your smartass remarks.'

'Yes,' said Rudy to Django. 'Like you and your mom.'

'We don't hit any little white balls,' said Django.

'OK,' said Rudy. 'My mistake. Sorry.'

The road took us along high cliffs. Far down below, the surf crashed on the rocks. We rounded the top of West Maui and drove a couple of miles, then Rudy pulled over and we got out of the car. Even seeing someone in a film standing on top of a tall building makes me tingle from the feet upwards; I wished we were watching for whales from a boat and I held on to Django's hand. 'There's Kahakuloa Head,' said Rudy. It was a huge rough rock less than a mile away, grey and ugly and it began to grow larger in my eyes the way things do when you approach over water. Then it froze like a photograph and I froze too: I couldn't speak, couldn't move. My hand was empty. I looked around for Django, heard him say, 'Another door', saw the blur of his T-shirt, then he wasn't there. A hump-back whale surged up out of the water off Kahakuloa Head and fell back with a sound like a thunderclap and a tower of spray.

Again and again I live that moment and wonder what happened. Rudy said Django got too close to the edge and slipped. How could I have let go of his hand? Death is such a big thing and he was such a small person.

'Right,' I said to myself, 'that's it for 1993 and our tenth-anniversary trip down Memory Lane. Now if we can return to 30 January, 2003 . . .'

This time I'd made my own arrangements. I hired a car at Kahului, drove to the Pioneer Inn, and checked myself in. I didn't want to see Rudy Ka'uhane. I was still full of anger, more at myself than at him. I couldn't help thinking that he ought not to have taken us to Kahakuloa but I was brought up against the fact that I'd made the decision not to go out on a boat.

This day in 2003 was the same kind of day as ten years ago, cool and grey. I followed the same road we'd taken in the Land Rover and in a very short time – I must have been driving faster than I thought – there I was looking at Kahakuloa Head and it was looking back at me with the face of the cyclops.

'You!' I said, recalling how when I first saw that painting at the Royal Academy I had to throw up. Now my eyes and my mind were no longer under my control and this grey and ugly rock was also being the Iao Needle and the black rock where the souls jumped off. I threw up again and leant against the car trying to pull myself together. 'What's the use?' I said. 'I'm the bad-luck woman.' I recited the names, leaving out *Badroulbadour* because I didn't know anyone on that boat: my stepfather Ron Burke; Dick Turpin; Sid Horstmann; Adam Freund; and Django. I wasn't going to add Elias's name to the list. My life was a thing where I had no place to stand any more. I looked at the edge where Django went over and said, 'Why not?' The cyclops, Kahakuloa Head, the Iao Needle and the black rock all nodded their approval.

'Do you mind?' I said as I heard Lucille sounding as if she needed a new silencer and a valve job. I wanted peace and quiet but I wasn't getting any. Now I was hallucinating Elias but he had a stronger grip than most hallucinations.

'Gotcha,' he said. Just like that. No emphasis. Here he was.

'You'll be sorry,' I said. 'I'm nothing but bad news.'

'As it happens,' he said, 'I've got good news.'

'I doubt it.'

'No, really, look at this.' He pulled a cutting from *The Times* out of his pocket. Picture of a Heinz tomato ketchup bottle standing on its head.

'So?' I said.

'After all these years they turned it around. Don't you see? Things don't just stay the same year after year.'

'You're crazy,' I said.

'Not enough yet but I'm working on it. I love you.'

'OK, I love you too, whatever that's worth.'

'It's worth everything,' he said, so I didn't argue with him.

38

THE TIMES

27 January 2003.

ENCORE

Jimmy Wicks, 60, guitarist, singer and songwriter with Mobile Mortuary, was pronounced dead of an apparent heart attack at his home in Clapton earlier today. In the ambulance taking him away, however, he sat up and said, 'Thanks for turning on the sound.' He subsequently underwent a triple bypass at Homerton Hospital and is now recovering in good spirits.

A NOTE ON THE AUTHOR

Russell Hoban is the author of many extraordinary novels including *Turtle Diary*, *Riddley Walker*, *Amaryllis Night and Day*, *The Bat Tattoo* and most recently *Her Name Was Lola*. He has also written some classic books for children including *The Mouse and his Child* and the *Frances* books. He lives in London.

A NOTE ON THE TYPE

The text of this book is set in Bembo, which was first used in 1495 by the Venetian printer Aldus Manutius for Cardinal Bembo's *De Aetna*. The original types were cut for Manutius by Francesco Griffo. Bembo was one of the types used by Claude Garamond (1480–1561) as a model for his Romain de L'Université, and so it was a forerunner of what became the standard European type for the following two centuries. Its modern form follows the original types and was designed for Monotype in 1929.